The Night
of the Bozos

The Night of the Bozos

by Jan Slepian

E. P. DUTTON • NEW YORK

Library of Congress Cataloging in Publication Data

Slepian, Jan.
  The night of the Bozos.

  Summary: Thirteen-year-old George and his Uncle Hibbie
were a team, a pair of loners separated from other people,
but the arrival of an extraordinary carnival girl changes
many things for both of them.
  [1. Emotional problems—Fiction. 2. Carnivals
—Fiction. 3. Interpersonal relations—Fiction]
I. Title.
PZ7.S6318Ni 1983 [Fic] 83-5564
ISBN 0-525-44070-4

Published in the United States by E. P. Dutton, Inc.,
2 Park Avenue, New York, N.Y. 10016

Published simultaneously in Canada by Clarke,
Irwin & Company Limited, Toronto and Vancouver

Editor: Julie Amper   Designer: Claire Counihan

Printed in the U.S.A.   COBE   First Edition
10 9 8 7 6 5 4 3 2 1

to Don—for obvious reasons

Chapter 1

His Uncle Hibbert swung the small delivery truck onto the dirt road that led to Mullin's Lake. It was a wonderfully warm June morning, and as George looked out at the narrow country lane and heard the soft brushing of the overhanging leaves on the roof of the van, it seemed to him the day was luminous with promise.

They soon came to a rise that circled the hill, and Hibbie leaned on the horn because of the blind curve ahead. The horn broke the comfortable silence between them and inspired Hibbie. "Almost there," he sang. "Almost there, almost there, almost there." The warning blast of the horn plus Uncle Hib's toneless refrain went through George's head like a dentist's drill. He pressed his eyes to flatten the noise, but said nothing. No sir, no complaints, not when they were just starting out.

The horn reminded him. "Hey Hib, we going to stop at the dump this afternoon? Remember you said?"

"Sure, kid." And because the sun was shining and because George was with him and because that came out so easy, he started singing again. "Surely, surely, surely, surely," he sang, leaping the scale in uneven steps. He held the last note as the turn ended, and there was the lake in the distance, like a picture on a postcard, as pretty as that.

Just then, the song broke off, and the brakes jammed on. Ahead of them, not twenty feet from the van, was a body crumpled up on the road. Holy cow, they could have run right over it!

For a big man, Hibbie was a fast mover. He was out of the truck before George got his own door open. They ran openmouthed, without a word, to where it lay sprawled in the dust.

Then . . . the body sat up. It smiled at them and said, "Guess I scared you some, huh?"

The girl jumped to her feet and fell to slapping her dress, front and back, to get rid of the dust of the road. All the time that she was bending and brushing, she didn't look at them. She brushed and slapped and talked in a rush while they stared at her like panting statues.

"I got so tired of walking, you can't believe. What's the matter with everybody around here? They scared or something? I've been walking and walking—all the way from town. You know, Mullin's Bridge? Funny name for a town. I've been walking, my thumb out to here, trying to get a lift, but nobody stops. You'd think I had a gun in my hand.

So when I heard your car coming, I had to do something a little extra, know what I mean? I heard about this trick of playing dead from someone, I don't know who. Probably someone."

She pointed to the distant lake with a trembling finger. The chatter stopped and more easily she said, "I just want to get there. Want to see the lake. Maybe go in the water."

She finally looked at them, and then she must have realized. "Hey," she said softly, in the high breathless way George had already fixed on, "did I do something dumb again? I guess I did, huh?"

Hibbie's face was still sweaty from the shock. "You could have gah-gah-gah-" He stopped. His throat closed on the sound, and he turned away.

George finished the sentence for him. "You could have got yourself killed pulling a trick like that! That was crazy!" The pounding of his heart slowed and outrage took over. Look at Uncle Hib—still pale with shock. There was nothing you could do with people like her. "C'mon, Uncle Hib. Let's go."

The girl cried, "Oh, oh, wait a minute." She flapped a helpless hand and stepped toward them, limping severely. "Ow! My ankle! I turned it back there, and now it hurts something awful. That's why I was so desperate. You can understand that, can't you?"

She turned to Hibbie, knowing somehow that he was the one. Ice cream on a hot day was firmer than Uncle Hib.

"Can't you just take me to the lake? I won't be any bother. I just want a ride is all. I'm really sorry about the scare. Honest I am. What do you say?"

She lifted her heavy dark hair from the back of her neck with a lazy arm, while deep, red brown eyes regarded Hibbie in a way that made George change his mind about how old the girl was. The little-girl voice was one thing, but the eyes said something else. He'd thought she was about his own age at first, thirteen, almost fourteen. But now he wasn't so sure, she was so changeable. What was sure was that she was going to get a ride with them.

Hibbie glanced at George first, checking the way they usually did. But then, without waiting for a sign, he nodded and smiled at her to say yes.

She stepped closer, and it was that moment, with the three of them standing on a country road, the sun on their heads and the girl between them, that George thought of as the beginning.

The girl pointed to a brown paper bag at the side of the road. "My stuff," she said, and limped to the car while Unc trotted over to get it. She climbed in next to Hibbie and settled the bag between her legs. "What's back there?" she asked, turning to the back of the van.

"It's full of bread and cake," said George, uncomfortable with questions. Now that the quaking had stopped, the old awkwardness was taking over.

"What?" said the girl, leaning over to peer at him. "I couldn't hear you."

George shifted and spoke up. "It's full of bread and cake," he repeated. "Trays and trays of it back there. My uncle is a Dugan Man for the lake here. We deliver here."

"You, too? That your job too? You old enough for that?" She was serious, and George was enormously flattered that she could think so. Suddenly his customary guard dropped and his own sly devil prodded him. "Actually, my uncle works for *me*. I'm just here today to check up on him, see he does his job, report back to the boss, stuff like that."

4

"Come onnnn!"

"Well, I'm just helping out for the summer. This is my first day."

George rolled his window all the way down while they were talking, because all of a sudden there was a definite smell in the van and it wasn't cake. Something—well, just a trace, but what was it?—like a zoo almost. Like a zoo and cotton candy both. Must come from the girl, but that kind of perfume doesn't come from a bottle. He leaned against the door so he could get a better look at what they had with them.

Nothing like a zoo to see. He once went on a trip to New York City with his mother's friend Carol, who took him to see the show at Radio City Music Hall. He saw ballet dancers all in white. For him, it was music turned solid, and the delicate aery dancers still frilled his dreams now and again. Those slender dancers returned to him now as he looked at the girl. Something in the way the mass of black hair was pulled back and held, something in the body held straight, something in the delicate pale face all bones and angles. Her blue checked dress with the round white collar was plain enough for Sunday School, and the sneakers on her feet were like everyone else's. Yet, there was something about her that said she wasn't from around here or any place he knew, and it wasn't just the smell.

His uncle caught his eye and flicked his head toward the girl.

"My uncle wants to know where you're from," said George.

"Can't he ask?" she said, touching Hibbie's arm, turning to him.

"No." She didn't have to know about Hibbie.

A flush rose to the pale cheeks, and she said, "I'm from over the fairgrounds. I'm with the Carnival there." She glanced sidelong at George with a slight smile, as if she knew what the words would do to him. Sure enough, George was dazzled.

"Didn't you know about the Carnival? We're doing a still date."

"A what?"

"It's when we set down someplace to make some money before we join up with a real fair. We're just the carny part, the rides and freaks and shows, not the 4-H's and all the farm stuff and animal auctions and all. Know what I mean? After next week we go to New Paltz, where we join up with a big one. I think your fire department sponsored us. I'm not really sure. We're just carnival. You know what that is? You ever been to a carnival?" the smile still on her lips, suddenly teasing.

When neither answered she said, "I'm Eula Lee Jeffers. Only you can call me Lolly like everyone else. That's how I called myself when I was a kid, and it stuck. Eula Lee, Lolly, get it?" She laughed aloud as if she'd said a joke, and right then George decided her voice was between singing and sighing, sexy as his dreams, like Marilyn Monroe in the movies.

"Lolly, Lolly," chanted Hibbie. He could say it easy. He shone with delight. "Lolly."

She waited expectantly.

"I'm George. George Weiss. This is my Uncle Hibbie. Hibbert Whipple."

Lolly asked Hibbie, "You a football player?" Then she turned from one to the other and said, "You don't look related, you know? You don't look anything like." She took in George, hands pressed between his thighs as if he didn't know where to put them, the black shock of hair almost hiding the wary eyes, small body next to her, tense, careful not to touch, nothing given away. And then over to Hibbie, who grabbed the wheel with meaty hands as solid as the rest of him, all sandy hair and frank, friendly eyes giving away everything. She said again, "You're nothing like. You sure you're related? I never heard of an uncle and a nephew so close in age anyway. You could be brothers. I have an aunt in Florida, but she's old as the hills. You kidding me?"

George smiled. And when the girl saw it, she warmed as if the sun came out. "Saaay! You should smile more often! It changes you altogether!"

He wanted to change the subject. "Your folks own it? The Carnival, I mean." He got the full force of her eyes. Dark like cellos, they were.

"My folks own . . . ? Oh, no," she said very seriously. "My dad owns Jeffers Jungle." She looked at George as if he should know something. "Haven't you ever heard of Jeffers Jungle?"

He shook his head as if hypnotized, waiting for the next surprise to come out of her mouth. What was Jeffers Jungle, some TV show? He could only think of Tarzan.

"My father says there's no one like us in any carnival in the whole world. We own the Wrestling Chimps."

"Oh," said George, as noncommittally as possible. Should he have heard of them too? Chimps. No wonder she smelled a little like a zoo.

"And you can have them," she added with a short mocking laugh.

And then they were at the Clubhouse. Hibbie parked in front of the large wooden building that stood guard over the small patch of gray sand where all the lake people went to swim.

There were two workmen from town standing in the shallow water, workclothes still on, putting up a diving board.

"Hey, see that, Hib? They got the diving board!" The two of them had worked the lights and music for the Improvement Gala last summer, to raise the money for it. George felt as if he owned some part of it. "Let's get on it sometime, okay?"

Just as he expected, his uncle pursed his lips doubtfully, but couldn't say no outright.

"Aw, come on," George said seriously. "The two of us could hold hands and jump in. Both together. With what you weigh, the lake will overflow; people will think a tidal wave hit them." He could always make Hibbie laugh.

Then Lolly chimed in, "They'll run screaming out of their houses, grabbing at kids, bankbooks, underwear, everything soaking wet. . . ."

Hibbie's high giggle was contagious.

George yelped, "And you know who they'll see standing in the dry lake?"

Lolly took the ball. "You and Hibbie and the other poor fish."

This really finished Hibbie. He pounded the wheel, laughter taking him over completely. She had no idea that she had just then entered private property, trespassed in a way that left George feeling vaguely miffed.

Hibbie radiated pleasure. "How about we p-p-pick you

up later. When we are fff— are through delivering. Want a lift back?"

"Hey, great!" she said, and as if they had known one another for years instead of minutes, she added, "You take me back to the fairgrounds, and I'll show you around."

George opened his door and jumped down from the truck. Lolly followed, and Hibbie came around to lean on a fender. The midmorning sun had already warmed and filled the beach. The small slide that pipelined screaming children into the water was busy and the air filled with their cries and splashings. George lost himself in the layers of sounds that seemed to need so many tracks to follow, from screech of humans to thud of workman's hammer.

He heard his name. It was Mr. Young, the manager of the Clubhouse, standing on the porch with a wrench in his hand. He looked like an aged Boy Scout. "I'll give you boys a call about the Gala next Saturday. That be all right with you?"

George nodded to him.

"Tell him again," Hibbie said to Lolly. "He w-wasn't listening."

"I only said I'll show you around, probably meet my folks, maybe some others; there's always open house around there. That's what I said."

Carefully George said, "That's okay. You drop me off home, Hib. I got things to do home. You go if you want. I got things to do."

Hibbie turned reproachful eyes to George and then said to Lolly, "We'll p-pick you up, take you home at least, if you're still here b-b-b-by the time we finish up."

She reached into the truck for her bag, and that's when George saw it. How did he miss it before? There on her arm, practically falling out of her sleeve, was a bright tattoo. Where other people had a vaccination, she had some kind of big flower like nothing George had ever seen before. A gorgeous red and yellow flower tattooed right there on her arm.

Chapter 2

He could hardly wait to get back into the truck and on their way so he could explode. "You see that, Hib? On her arm? On sailors maybe. On rough guys who work on the waterfront, lifting thousands of pounds . . . maybe. On the *marines,* for crying out loud. Who else has a tattoo, Hib? Ever see one on a girl before? Come on, tell the truth. A weirdo, right? What do you say?"

Hibbie let George talk until they rounded that end of the lake, out of sight of the bathers, and then pulled over to the side of the road. He hooked his elbow over the back of his seat to lean closer. Puzzlement and concern shone through his whole bearing like light through a window. "What's the m-m-matter with you, George? How could you say no to that? How come you say no all the time?" He raised a helpless hand and let it drop. "Here we have this chance— anyone else would jump at such a thing. Shown around a carnival from the inside, and okay, so m-m-m-maybe we have to meet some p-p-p-people, say hello. What's the big deal? If *I* can, you can. But first thing out of your mouth is bang, no. All the time, no. It worries your ma, and it worries me."

"What are you talking about? I don't say no all the time!" burst George. Why did Hibbie have to spoil the day! He didn't want to hear this. It was the girl!

"You don't? Listen George, I know you since before you were born, right? I've lived with you all your life, and I'm telling you that more and more that's w-what you do—like just now. I wasn't going to bring this up, because God knows you hear it enough from your mother. B-b-but gee, kid, what are you bucking for? All-American Hermit?"

George's mouth twitched at the idea. He had a brief flash of himself crawling out of a cave covered with spiderwebs and animal skins. The club over his shoulder was to bash anyone who came close.

Then the unfairness of what Hibbie had said overcame him. What did he mean, *hermit?* Didn't they have each other? That's no hermit if you have someone!

"Aw, Mom worries too much over nothing!" He looked up hopefully at his uncle for agreement. He wanted Hibbie back where they were, the two musketeers against the rest.

In his ears he could hear his mother's tender treble, like the sad vibrato of his guitar. "Georgie Porgie, what am I going to do with you? It's not good for you to be alone so much, so wrapped up in one thing. Music isn't the world.

Up in your room fussing with it all the time! Not a friend in the world except your uncle, and I declare you're just birds of a feather. Oh, if only your father were still alive!" And then she would be off on how tragic it was that he never knew his own father and cursing all wars.

With his mother's soft, mournful voice in his ears, Hibbie's sharpness jolted him. "No, no, you're wrong there," the big man said. "That's what I'm trying to t-t-tell you. This isn't nothing! Know what my poor sister said to me last thing when we put her on the train this morning?"

George couldn't look at him. He shook his head dumbly.

His mother was a nurse and was often called away on a private case to make some extra money, leaving them for days, sometimes a week or more at a time. She always said Hibbie was a born baby-sitter, and that their mother had had him as a blessed afterthought, just so he could come live with her and help out. Calling his Uncle Hibbie a baby-sitter always made them laugh, but it was true that Hib was the one who looked after him when she was gone. All his life. No, he didn't know what his mother had said to Hib that morning, but he could guess. All he remembered at the station was the familiar clutch of love and loss he always felt when she had to leave. He wanted to cling when she kissed him good-bye, and at the same time was in an itch to be away, starting this job, alone with Hib.

Hibbie said, "She made me promise you wouldn't hole up in your room all the time. All excited she was, about you making my rounds, thinking you might get out of yourself, make a friend. And I promised her right there and then. I said to her, 'Joanie, we'll get him to join the human race yet. Don't you worry,' I said. You were right *there*, George. Didn't you hear?" His smile was rueful. "No, you were probably listening to the train tracks. Well, now l-l-look at you. Pulling in. Avoiding. Saying no. Saying no to a swell invitation like that!"

George lifted liquid eyes to his uncle, and Hibbie shook his head and said very gently, "What's the matter, kid?" He passed his hand across George's cheek. "You afraid if you lift your head, someone will take a potshot at it? Is that why you turn off other kids?"

This stung. Hotly, George cried, "Look who's talking about potshots! Haven't they taken enough at you? Besides, what other kids? Listen, they're as interested in me as I am in them. You think I want to sit around and talk baseball scores? I got something better to do! Anyhow, when's the last time *you* went out? *You* can't talk!"

Hib let the air out of his lungs and flung his head back. "You know why that is. I've got something gives people the willies to listen to me. Makes 'em go all goo-goo-eyed with embarrassment. So I give them a break. I keep out of their way. What's the comparison? They're giving *me* the finger, but with you it's the other way around. Hey, you're just starting out. You gotta get out there, kid. That's where the action is, not in your room with the music going."

Then he grinned, although his eyes were still anxious. He started up the van again. "What a pair we are, hey, George? Some twosome. Gruesome twosome."

"Yeah, a couple of coconuts." They laughed together, and then things were all right between them again. Something still sat heavy on George's chest. "Hibbie, you remember you promised me we could go to the dump after? You promised, and all of a sudden we're not going. You're busy making dates with that girl." A piece of ammunition leaped to

14

his mind. "And you know what? Something I bet you didn't see. Remember she had such a bad ankle we had to give her a lift? Well, just now, back there, when she walked away, she didn't limp anymore. That's who you're making dates with."

Hibbie shook his head and got them rolling again. "Okay, kid. That's enough. And here I thought it was you two getting along so well. What we're going to do is, you want to go to the dump? We go. But first we pick up Lolly. Then we stop at the dump. *Then* we all go to the Carnival and let Lolly show us around. That's it!"

The subject was dropped and work began. The houses were scattered around the lakefront, hidden by hedges and bushes along the road they traveled. Sometimes there was a gap in the hedge like a peephole, so that George had a quick glimpse of the lake with piers that sat on the water like arrows on a map, pointing to the graceful houses at the edge. Sometimes only a mailbox told of a nearby driveway. On the water side, the driveway was a sharp dip down to the garage; on the other side, the van had to climb upwards to get to the house, like climbing the side of a bowl. Up and down they drove, all around the lake.

Ladies smiled at them out their back doors. "Why, hello there, Hibbie. Who's this?" they asked. "My, I wouldn't have thought you old enough to have such a big boy for a nephew. You're just a boy yourself." Hibbie looked old enough to George to have Moses for a nephew: He was already twenty-three.

"What's the special for the day?" asked the ladies. Usually Hibbie handed them a printed card, but today George rattled off, "Coffee cake, ma'am. Maple walnut."

They worked their way around the lake, emptying the trays of wrapped goods, seeing a lot of back doors.

By midafternoon, they rounded the lake and headed for the Clubhouse to pick up Lolly.

She was sitting on a rock on the other side of the road, her back to the racket on the beach, small and solitary. Her dress was tucked under her knees, hands clasped in her lap like a good schoolgirl. No one in the world could guess about her, George thought. No one could guess carnival or tattoos.

Opposite, the small spread of sand was covered with mothers and little kids. Over near the new diving board was a flock of girls flirting with the lifeguard, laughing and pushing and teasing and showing off for him. George could hear their voices—like birds, like flutes. A volleyball game was in progress on the grass near the Clubhouse. He recognized some of the kids from his class, leaping and jumping for the ball like fish at bait. He had a flash of envy for their smooth and willing muscles. His own were so unreliable. They made him the last chosen when he was forced into a game in gym class. They made him dread the ropes and that stupid vaulting horse. Then he hated himself for even caring. He could play the piano like nobody's business, and they didn't even know. His fingers were more nimble; they worked better than theirs ever would. So who cared about volleyball?

But he felt an unexpected surge of feeling for Lolly, sitting there forlorn, looking off like she was alone in a room.

Hibbie honked the horn. Lolly looked up and saw them. So did a bunch of little children on the beach. They came running, crying, "Hibbie! Hibbie!" He climbed down from the van and was surrounded by kids in bathing suits, rubber tubes around their middles, wet or sandy or both. All had their hands outstretched like beggars. "Hibbie, Hibbie, got something for us?" The ones in the rear jumped up to be seen, like baby birds waiting to be fed.

Hibbie reached in and under his seat. From a squashed box, he distributed pieces of cupcake.

"Stale," he announced to George and Lolly as if apologizing.

Once more Lolly climbed between them.

"Go swimming?" asked Uncle Hib.

"You bet," said Lolly in her high, breathy way. "I'm a terrific swimmer. Won medals and all."

George could swear he still got a whiff of zoo, and her hair wasn't wet. But mainly he thought that when he had his tape recorder, he would search her out and get that voice nailed down for his collection.

He had to ask. "Say, what is that tattoo on your arm?" He tried to sound casual, as if it were no big thing, everyone had tattoos.

She clasped her arm quickly, and once again a flush rose to the pale face. "Isn't it beautiful? It's a hibiscus flower."

"A what?"

"A hibiscus, a gorgeous flower that grows in the tropics. I have a calendar home with a picture of Hawaii on it and a beautiful girl standing there with this kind of flower in her hair. So I got Wilson to do it on me. Have you seen it?" she asked Hibbie. She squirmed around in her seat so that she was kneeling on it like a little kid. She held out her arm so Hibbie could get a good look. It was a strange sight on that thin arm, a deep red, welling like blood, a long yellow stem growing out of the flower like an antenna.

Hibbie glanced down quickly and said, "Mmmmm," as if he had been shown something good to eat.

This satisfied her, and she sat back to examine it more closely herself, pressing it as if testing for ripeness. "Ooooh, did this hurt at first! My arm was out to here."

George could imagine what his mom would say if he came home with that. "*Where's the ax? I'm going to chop your arm off!*" He wondered if carnival people could be so different. "Didn't your parents mind?" he asked.

"No, no, my folks didn't mind at all. My mother doesn't care one way or the other, and Pop thinks it's great, just great." She laughed at some inner vision and said, "You should have seen the look on those faces back there at the lake when they got a load of this. It got some notice, I can tell you."

George and Hibbie exchanged a wild glance. Imagine being looked at like that. Wanting it.

Hibbie spoke up then. "How c-c-c-come you did it?"

"How come? I wanted to. I love it! I did it a couple of weeks ago when I first came up."

"Up?"

"Uh-huh. From Gibbtown. Gibbtown, Florida? I stay with my Aunt Eva, used to be a cooch girl, but now she's retired. Poor her, right? I stopped traveling around on account of school. At least that's my folks' story. Privately, I think they just wanted me out of their hair." She shrugged as if who cares. "Well, I got Wilson, the Bozo, to do it. He's going to be a real artist someday, and I told him I would be his first show. He's going to do the rest of me just like Miss Wilma Pugmire. She's wonderful. She's the Tattooed Lady. You'll meet her probably if you stay. You going to stay?"

George mutely nodded yes. Then he heard something. "Shush!" he said. "Stop the car a minute, Hib." He stuck his head out the window, closed his eyes and held his body like a wire tensing for current. Sounds filtered into the van: children's calls, birdsong, the rustle of leaves. And then overhead there was the drone of a plane, swelling and receding like a breath.

"A flat," said George, opening his eyes and pulling his head back in.

"We have a flat!" cried Lolly.

"The plane," said George patiently. "The sound of it. A flat. A, B, C, D, like in music."

Lolly stared and giggled and then put her hand over her mouth as if she regretted what had slipped out.

"What's with him?" she asked Hibbie.

They were back on the highway headed for town.

"N-n-nothing." Hibbie smiled at the road ahead. "That's all he thinks of—his music. That's why we have to stop at the dump."

Chapter 3

As soon as they drove down the gravel road to the dump, George's pulse began to jump.

Hibbie stopped before the shed. "When do you want to be picked up? And have a heart, George. Lolly here wants to get home."

"No, no," Lolly said quickly. "Don't mind me." She stared over at the piles of garbage in disbelief and then at George, who had jumped out and was rapidly changing into hiking shoes. He had already pulled on dirty long pants over his shorts. On his belt hung canvas gloves, a small crescent wrench, pliers, wire cutters and a pair of tin snips. It was his dump outfit.

"You look like you're going to operate," she said to George. "Do you take out appendixes, too?"

He was in one big itch to get going, no time to fool around. "An hour, Hib. That's all I need. Give me an hour."

Hibbie mimicked him. " 'An hour,' he says, 'that's all,' he says." He couldn't hide his amusement and pride, though he pretended irritation. "Can you imagine being in this d-d-dump for an hour?" he said to Lolly.

"Not even for two seconds," she answered.

"Tell you what. We'll go back to the b-b-bakery and unload. That okay with you, Lolly? Then we'll be back to pick you up at"—he checked his watch—"four thirty on the nose. Got that? You be ready, George."

The van turned around, and George bounded to the shed. He began to smile and then to sing wordlessly. Everywhere he looked pleased him. Everything he saw was rich with possibilities.

As usual, Sam and Leland were leafing through their comic books and listening to the radio that sat between them on the grimy floor. Some time ago, George had rescued the radio from the dump and fixed it up to give to them. He restored toys for their kids. On the shelf behind Leland was a small fan George had found and fixed for them last month for the summer heat. In return, they gave him precious permission to rummage freely through the piles and take home what he wanted.

As caretakers, their duties weren't heavy. Every car had to stop at their shed to be identified as belonging to a resident and directed to the right pile to dump its stuff. Once in a while the men had to climb on the bulldozers that sat out on the field like great yellow beasts set out to graze. These bulldozers pushed the junk into manageable and neat piles when the spillover got to be too much. But otherwise there was nothing much to do except throw stones at the rats, read, and stay mildly drunk. George thought they had wonderful jobs.

"Hi, Sam. Hi, Leland. Got anything for me?" They knew to put aside what was interesting or odd for him to look at.

"Look what the wind blew in. Hi there, George. Anything for our man, Lee?"

Leland didn't raise his head. Just shook it.

"Any fresh loads?" Sometimes a truck would dump wonderful things. Last week, he had found a load of plastic labels like credit cards, imprinted for scientific equipment. He didn't know what he would do with them yet, but they were home in a carton on a shelf.

"Naw, nothing new, is there, Lee?" Leland didn't answer. He was the grumpy one, and Sam was talky. What were Hibbie and Mom complaining about? These guys were his good friends!

"Go on, baby, get to work," said Sam, grinning.

"Can I climb up?" asked George. Most of the time, they didn't let him climb on the shed roof. Said it was dangerous. Bad enough they let him fool around in their dump; that was dangerous, too.

"No, sir!" said Sam, teasing.

"Let him," rumbled Leland, still buried in his comics.

Before their minds could change, George was up and on the roof of the shed, his favorite lookout. From there he could see what was what and organize himself.

He stood and gazed. He took a deep breath and let it out slowly.

Spread before him was mound after mound of dump stuff,

22

piled fifteen to twenty feet high. They covered several acres of arid burned-out ground, like dunes on a desolate planet.

This was his domain. Except for his room at home, it was here that he felt most competent. It was here that he had the eye of a Moroccan horse trader. No siren's song could be sweeter than the piled trash in front of him. It held treasure only he could spot. It was he, George Weiss, the cringer, the hider, the . . . what was it Hibbie had called him? The All-American Hermit? It was he who could sift through that garbage with one shrewd, calculating glance and light on the one perfect gem.

He had to get to work. At once he was all business. No time to lose. An hour was never enough. He checked the mounds one after the other and decided which of them to head for first.

As he trotted, the old sense of excitement and expectation rose and enveloped him like a cloud. At the same time, he had to be careful not to step in garbage juice, unnameable stuff that gave the dump its special aroma.

Head in the clouds, feet dealing with muck, he climbed up one of the mounds to yank out a broken half of lawn mower. He deftly removed the motor and then spotted an electric kitchen clock nearby with an intact second hand. Good. Very useful. They both went on the take-home pile at the bottom of the mound.

Then his eye fell on a pile of fluorescent tubes, sticking up from the debris like the bones of some old carcass. He couldn't resist. He'd never get around to checking all the piles at this rate, but then again, a heap of fluorescent tubes all intact didn't come along every day. He lined them up like soldiers and at just the right angle broke a few with a table leg. Because of the vacuum inside, they imploded with a very satisfactory pop. A pop and a tinkle at the same time. George heard it more as a shimmering in the air, and he listened to the fadeaway with a pleasure he would never be able to describe.

As he listened, it seemed necessary to him to expand what he had just heard. Quickly he gathered up a handful of old nuts and bolts and nails scattered at his feet and tossed them high in the air above him. He bashed another fluorescent tube. The pop and the fadeaway of the tube was then followed by a rain of clicks, pocks, tonks, and clanks as the metallic bric-a-brac bounced off the side of a baby carriage, a piece of wood, a discarded TV. For a moment he had created a mini-symphony of noises, noises as separate and distinct as voices.

Why the sounds of life around him meant so much to him, he didn't know. They interested him. They were the building blocks of a kind of music alive only in his head or in his inspired fooling, like just now. That kind of music wasn't to be heard on his record player or in what he played on the piano. Once in a long while on the radio, he heard something called electronic music which came close. What he knew was that the sounds he could wring from ordinary things were not unchangeable, but were like clay or plastic, his to bend and shape as he wished, his to play with. The world was full of things to feed his fascination, from the sweet clunk of a hammer on car springs to strange sounds locked up in electricity. All his—and let the rest go hang.

"Hey, what are you doing up there?"

A boy about his own age stood below, grinning up at him.

"Nothing much."

His white T-shirt and chino pants weren't dump clothes.

Behind him, a man was unlocking the back of a station wagon, getting ready to unload.

"You allowed to hang around here? I thought no one could."

George shrugged. He didn't want to say. Might get Sam and Lee in trouble, but he was sure tempted to tell this kid he was the only one, the only one allowed.

"Mark! Get a move on. Let's go!" The man was impatient. He tossed a carton from the car to the ground with a grunt of distaste.

"Gotta go now. The old man'll kill me." The boy gestured with a thumb.

George's expert eye swept over the back of the wagon. It was filled with high-class throw-out stuff, what he called money trash.

"Want some help unloading?" he asked. It was the perfect opportunity to get the first look, the first pickings.

"Hey Dad, we got us some help."

The man in the red checked shirt and dark-rimmed glasses scratched his beard as he looked George over cautiously. "Why, much obliged there. Very nice of you. Mark, you and your friend here unload the rest of this junk while I speak to the men in the office."

George almost burst out laughing. That's a good one. *Office.* Sam and Leland would love that.

"Wouldn't you know he'd get out of it somehow?" said Mark, looking after his father, amusement and scorn on his long, full-lipped face.

The two boys worked together, tossing the slats of a crib on the pile, unloading the stained and torn mattress, a carton of sewing material, a broken hassock.

A box of old tennis balls was next. "Bet you can't hit that

stick up there." Mark pointed to the handle of an upright vacuum cleaner sticking out of the mound, almost to the top. The boy squinted at the target, took aim, and threw the ball with that quick, expert snap of the wrist that told George he was one of those. Probably captain of the team. He didn't hit the stick, but his ball sailed right over it.

George knew he could *fly* up there faster and easier than he could reach it with his from-the-shoulder heave.

"Nah, that's no fun. Hey, I'll show you something."

He looked around urgently and spotted a couple of large round tubes on the ground, big cylinders that rugs were once packed in. They had rolled down from the mound. Mark watched in silence as George picked up a wide board and brought it down on one end of each tube, denting them somewhat.

"Now listen to this," he said to Mark. He whacked the other end and listened with satisfaction to the deep clunk each made, though one was slightly higher in pitch than the other. Anyone could see that with a set of those you could make a xylophone. "Hear that?" he said eagerly. Who could resist?

"Yeah," said Mark. "Nice. My kid brother has a toy he bangs something like that." He turned back to the car. "Let's dump the rest of this crap. Maybe go exploring. I hear there are rats here. We could take potshots."

George let Mark unload alone while he poked through a carton of miscellaneous junk. Suddenly his fingers stopped sifting. He stared at what he had uncovered, not believing his eyes. A real honest-to-goodness push-button doorbell. So hard to find! He'd been searching for ages because he needed just one more, and here it was. He grabbed it and pocketed it in a flash. At that very moment, the car-horn organ, the newest and best instrument that he had ever invented, was sitting on his worktable in his room, waiting for this very push button. It was a great day after all. George had what he wanted. A practiced look at what was left in the car told him there was nothing more for him here. Mark was emptying the box of tennis balls by taking aim at various targets up and down the mound. "Bang!" he cried. "Powie," he said, as the balls landed like bullets.

"So long. I gotta go now."

"See you around," said Mark vaguely.

George decided where he would head for next and moved away without another word or look at the car or Mark.

Before he was out of earshot, Mark's father returned.

"Who was that?" he gestured at the intent back.

"Nobody," said the boy, taking aim at another target.

Time sped by for George. He had collected his findings in piles at the foot of the mounds and was lost in fantasy as he leafed through a carton of what he called death stories. These were the memorabilia, the pictures, papers and belongings once so terribly precious to someone alive and now junk for the junkyard. He wove whole lives from pictures of long-ago children and from inscriptions in books. He heard songs in his head from glossies of pop stars from another age, and dreamed events for the funny getups in discarded family albums. He was deep into the refuse of another life when he heard Hibbie's horn blow. He must have been honking quite a while, because he was leaning on it. Hib was now in his own jalopy, a '55 Chevy whose side door was held on to the car by a rope.

George waved. Hib knew what to do.

Now was the time of agonizing decision. Slowly Hibbie

drove from mound to mound while George trotted alongside, telling him when to stop and where to go next. There was only the trunk and backseat to fill, and George had to choose, had to leave some of those precious things behind. And once left behind they were never to be recovered. It was an awful time for him and yet, driving off, he looked back at what he had salvaged, felt in his pocket for the doorbell push button and knew what Midas must have felt when he counted his gold.

Chapter 4

The Carnival sat in Smith's field, just over the covered bridge.

Where were the freaks, the girlie shows, the games? George had supposed crowds and music, movement and color. A carnival in the daytime was something else, something sadder. It all looked a little seedy and rundown. The Ferris wheel looked rickety in the strong sunshine, and the merry-go-round needed a paint job. Faded canvas fringed the stalls, flapping once bright colors in the soft breeze. Stray dogs were everywhere, sniffing at the empty cups flattened along the midway or at the candy wrappers fluttering against the wires that held down the game and food stands. George noticed a drunk sleeping it off in the weeds between the stalls and thought the whole Carnival looked a little like that. Some people were strolling about, but not many. A few mothers were pulling at small arms, pulling their children home. A few boys and girls, arms entwined, holding enormous stuffed animals, were headed for their cars. It was the tail end of a weekday afternoon, and most things were closed, the flaps down, waiting, as if resting for the night.

George and Hibbie walked the midway looking around them. It was like visiting a ghost town. Every few steps, they had to wait for Lolly. Once she was stopped by an official-looking man in a white shirt and black bow tie who bent to shake a finger at her. She was greeted by a dark angry woman closing a fortune-telling booth. She darted in and out of the trailers parked on the grass in back of the booths. Once, while Lolly and Hibbie waited, George stepped up to the test-your-own-strength stand. It was unmanned, and the big sledgehammer rested on a box like a toy waiting to be played with. He looked up at the high pole with the bell on top and decided he would send the wooden block smashing right up to that bell, right up to where it said Superman. He lifted the sledgehammer and staggered backwards, managing to drop it before it sent him sprawling. He looked at his soft arm with disgust. "Hey Hibbie, c'mon, you do it!" Unc could send that thing flying right past the bell and on the way to Mars. Hibbie shook his head. He didn't want to, didn't have to, never showed off.

Lolly led them away from the midway, cutting across the field. She pointed ahead to two large vans completely apart from the Carnival core, but clearly in the most important spot in the lot, as if having a stage all to themselves. "We're going over there," she said. "That's where I live. That's Jeffers Jungle."

As they neared the vans, George knew it wasn't supper he smelled. As a matter of fact, downwind, it was enough to drain his sinuses. So this was home-sweet-home to Lolly. He felt the old rush of silliness. He could picture it. *"Hi honey, I'm home. What's that funny smell?"*

"You know those buzzards who ate that dead cow? They just sicked up on your bed."

As they neared the trailers, a thickset man emerged from one of them and tossed a pail of something out the door. George didn't like to think of what. The man held up a hand in salute to Lolly. "Find that lake you were so set on?" he called to her. His nod included them all. "Your ma's been waitin' on you to set the table. Company comin'." He walked to them like a man in pain. His mouth was full of strong white teeth, and there wasn't a fleck of gray in the thick patch of black hair. Yet up close his face was old, full of little white scars, like the cross-stitching on the tablecloths George's mom was fond of doing. Lolly introduced them to her father, Mr. Jeffers. After shaking hands, he threw back his head and hollered, "Marjorie!"

A large redheaded lady stepped out of the trailer carrying a hairy bundle in her arms. The bundle moved, and George was captivated to see a baby chimp with its eyes closed, as content as an infant with its mother. The makeup was thick on the woman, lavender lips, false eyelashes like fringed rugs, gold wheels hanging from her ears. She was wearing bright red pedal pushers that looked as if they would split like a melon if she so much as leaned.

31

"Evenin' all," she said. "Who have we here?" Her voice reminded George of Hibbie's car horn. She looked Hibbie up and down like a shopper.

Hibbie got stuck on the "Pleased to meet you," and as he stuttered his greeting, a certain kind of interest drained from her eyes as if a plug had been pulled.

She turned her attention to her daughter, and her genial manner changed entirely. "Shake it, Lolly. Where ya been? You're never here when I need you. We're settin' up out here. The Threshams are comin' with the new baby, and so is Miss Wilma and Edgar Dawes. Your father invited the new Bozo, but he may be takin' over supper hour. Set a place anyhow."

She was a great deal friendlier in a hearty rough way when she spoke to George and Hibbie, who were standing at embarrassed attention. "You some new friends of my girl?" Suspicion entered. To Lolly, she said, "Where did you meet, I'm askin'?"

Lolly's manner was coaxing. "Mama, George and Hibbie were so nice! They gave me a ride to that lake and then brought me back and all. I'd told them I'd show them around."

"Much obliged," Mrs. Jeffers said to them. "If it won't be interferin' with plans, you fellas are welcome to take dinner with us. There's plenty." She bent over the baby chimp. "Joey's goin' to like that, aren't you sweetheart?" She kissed the animal on the mouth.

Lolly's whole face brightened. "Stay, why don't you? Can you? I told you there was open house around here."

George threw an anguished glance at Hibbie. Cold fingers moved inside him and touched off a slight nausea. He had trouble lifting his eyes to Mrs. Jeffers. How was he going to sit at the table with a whole bunch of strangers? And here was Hibbie jumping in with both feet when he should be the one . . .

"Thanks. We w-w-w-will," Hibbie said for both of them. George promised himself that later he would kill him dead.

Lolly went off with her mother, and Mr. Jeffers said, "Come on, I'll show you Jeffers Jungle, and I guarantee you never seen anything like it in your entire life."

He unlocked the back of one of the vans, and George thought his nose would fall off. Up close, the van had a pong that could fell an ox. Hibbie turned a shade of green, and George became an instant mouth breather. Mr. Jeffers noticed and laughed. "Guess it gets a little high around here. I don't notice it no more." Cages lined the dark inside, and from them issued grunts and snuffles, primitive noises from the start of time. Mr. Jeffers picked up a bucket of what might have been fruit once upon a time, say about the Middle Ages. He said, "You get used to everything in this life, and good honest animal stink is better than some, I can tell you." He sniffed the air as if it were fresh bread. The floor was slippery, and when Mr. Jeffers turned on the overhead light, George could see why it was. "Watch out underfoot," chuckled Mr. Jeffers, as if the patties strewn here and there were some adorable toys one shouldn't break.

"Suppertime!" he announced to the cages, and all hell broke loose. The yips and squeals were for the black dripping bananas, shapeless apples, rotted plums even flies wouldn't eat. George longed for a tape recorder.

Mr. Jeffers pointed to a small clump in the corner. "This here is Okra. My missus was holding her new little 'un Joey.

Say hello, Okra." Okra scratched her neck and made kissing noises in the air. "Ain't love grand?" said Mr. Jeffers. "My best fighter," he stated with pride. The chimp didn't look more than sixty pounds to George. He felt that, skinny as he was, he could wrestle a little thing like that. He could take care of her in nothing flat, even with muscles like pancakes. Okra picked up her dripping bowl and tossed a plum at George. Luckily he saw it coming and ducked. Then she stretched out a paw to Hibbie as if she wanted to hold hands. Hibbie was ready to hold hands with Okra all right, but was called over to the cage opposite.

"Over here is Trix. She and Dr. Pepper there get along fine, so we keep 'em together. Okra is jealous, aren't you girl?" Trix was busy in one corner of the cage piling up manure patties one on top of the other, like a kid playing with blocks. She looked up at the company, and grunted. Her roommate, Dr. Pepper, was wild, yipping and barking at the strangers, swinging on the rubber tube that hung from the top of the cage, leaping to the bars, then bounding back to the swing. The chimp calmed when his bowl was filled, and hunched over it, smelling and smacking, his little red eyes on the men constantly.

He looked so much like a suspicious old man that George burst out laughing. "Just like a person," he said.

"Well, if you think they're human, you've got another think coming." George had touched a nerve. Mr. Jeffers leaned against the bars of the cage and allowed Dr. Pepper to suck his hanging fingers. "No sir, they're not human, and I say so that knows more about these animals than most men alive. I've been workin' with 'em and had 'em in my own house growin' like my own. Some are mean and some are sweet. Some are smart and some are dumb. Jes' like people in some ways. But no sir, they're not human."

He looked down at the chimp who now had hold of Hibbie's hand, swinging on it, wanting to take it off of him. He pulled his fruit bowl over to the bars and tried to dip Hibbie's hand into it.

"He's taken quite a shine to you," said Mr. Jeffers, squinting up at Hibbie, the crosshatch lines in his face deeper for the smile. He squatted to scratch the chimp. "My wife now, she thinks they are. People I mean. Loves 'em to death and doesn't mind the mess. I think she likes 'em better'n her own. . . ."

He cleared his throat and moved on, stepping over to the next cage, larger than the others. A dark shape in the shadows moved and became a gorilla. He was twice the size of the chimps, but even so George was surprised that he wasn't all that big, not up to him even, and he wasn't the tallest in his class.

The darkness in the van and the strangeness of the surroundings allowed George to speak up. "They don't look so tough," he said to Mr. Jeffers. "I mean to fight. A grown man could do it easy, I bet. Even me. Well, not me, no sir. I don't fight anything that breathes. But if I did."

This seemed to strike Mr. Jeffers as very funny. "Why, you don't know what you're talkin' about, son. You've never seen a chimp in action, I'll put my purse on that. Greased lightnin'. Fastest gun in the West. Never know what hit you. You'll see. Stay for tonight, and you'll see. Hear that Li'l Sis? He thinks you're a lead-pipe cinch."

The gorilla leaned on his knuckles and looked them over with solemn eyes. Mr. Jeffers introduced them. "This here

is Li'l Sis. I wrestle him every night of my life, and I'm tellin'
you I'm gettin' too old for it. Yes sir, hear that, Li'l Sis?
You're gettin' too much for me. Here's your sumpin' special."

Li'l Sis was handed half a melon, but he wasn't interested.
He didn't take his eyes from the newcomers, especially Hibbie, who was making mouth noises at him and holding out
his hand through the bars as if it were a pussy cat in there
instead of a gorilla. Mr. Jeffers had to nudge Li'l Sis's hand
to get him to hang on to the melon. He took it, smelled it
and dropped it. Then he began to poke around in his belly
hairs as if there were a better dinner to be found there.

Mr. Jeffers grinned at them. "Maybe you don't know it,
but this creature you see here is one of the most ferocious
in all captivity. I'd have him roar for you, but I'll save his
voice for the marks tonight. I give 'em a choice, you see.
A choice every time. This gorilla here or one of my chimps.
They can freely pick either one to wrestle. And I'm here
to tell you, never once did poor Li'l Sis get chosen. Ain't
that right, sir?" he asked the busy gorilla. "So I get to wrestle
him instead, don't I? Whew. It's a wonder I'm alive to tell
you." He suddenly threw back his head in a short laugh.
"Yessirree, we have our secrets don't we, Li'l Sis?"

What secrets? George wondered. They go out on dates
together?

They had moved on and walked the length of the van to
stop in back of the driver's seat.

"You young fellas want to help me get ready for tonight?
You can give me a hand." They did indeed.

One whole side of the van was unhooked to form the floor
of the fighting ring. Hibbie and George set out thick
wooden stumps to rest it on. They were told to unroll a large

canvas from the top of the van to go over the ring. It made a kind of tent once the ridgepoles were in place. There was a flap opening in front so that only the paying customers could get in. "Like putting a circus together," George whispered to Hibbie. When they finished, Mr. Jeffers handed them large cardboard palm trees that had been stowed behind the cages to set around the ring outside the canvas. George and Hibbie backed off to get the effect, and it really looked like a jungle to them.

"B-b-b-beautiful," said Hibbie. Mr. Jeffers nodded. He knew it.

He unlocked the back of the van so it formed a platform to stand on. "My bally," he said. "Where I make my pitch, my sell. I bring out the chimps, let the marks see what's to fight, let 'em get a look at the competition. They think it's easy, too. Just like you there, young fella. Marks? Why they're payin' customers, son. Greatest people in the world. Marks are what comes to see us."

His name was shouted, like the honk of a goose.

"Be right there, Marge," he shouted back. "We're being asked for. Guess supper is ready."

He looked up at Hibbie, who just stood there like Li'l Sis, a quiet shape. "Say, you don't talk much, do you?"

George answered for him. "He stutters."

"So?"

Hibbie smiled his big sweet smile. "People," he said and then waved his hand as if that one word was explanation enough.

Mr. Jeffers paid no attention to that at all. He took hold of Hibbie's arm and whistled. "Say, young fella, how would you like to earn five bucks? Wrestle one of my chimps tonight? Forget Li'l Sis, take on the little fellas. Five dollars to anyone who can pin one down, and fifty cents more for each second you hold one down, both shoulders to the floor. How's that for handsome?"

Hibbie grinned and looked at George and raised both shoulders. He looked down and then up, shook his head, laughed a bit and then said yes.

Mr. Jeffers clapped him on the shoulder. "Well all right then. Let's go eat!"

Chapter 5

A long table was set up by the side of the other van, up-wind from Jeffers Jungle. It was covered by a white plastic cloth, and thick soup bowls marked the place settings. Long loaves of bread lined the middle of the table like felled logs.

Lolly stepped down from the van carrying a big black pot of something steamy. She looked around for George and Hibbie, and when she saw them approaching with her father, she smiled and held up the pot for them to see. Her shoulders bunched under the weight, her tattoo clearly visible. In this setting, George didn't think it looked so odd. She placed the pot in front of Mrs. Jeffers, who began to ladle out bowls of the chili while Joey, the baby chimp, clung to her shoulder.

There were some people there already, sitting around talking, easy and laughing, like family.

George took a deep breath at the sight of the busy table and longed to turn and run. "Sit here, George," said Mrs. Jeffers motioning to a nearby chair. "And you sit here, Hibbie." Mr. Jeffers had other plans. He led Hibbie by the sleeve to the other end of the table to sit with him. "He fights Okra tonight. We have things to talk about," he told his wife. George threw his uncle an imploring glance, but already Hib was listening to Mr. Jeffers, his earnest brow wrinkled with absolute attention.

"Meet the Threshams," boomed Mrs. Jeffers. Her voice made George's head buzz like an overloaded mike. He nodded at the kid sitting next to her, and the next instant the tips of his fingers turned cold as he realized it wasn't a kid. A grown man was sitting there! The body was regular size, but his legs were pegs sticking out of the immaculate shorts. He had no arms, no arms at all. Just stumps like flippers with fingers at the ends.

He waved one of the stumps at George and in a rich bass voice said, "Flippo, the Seal Boy, at your service, but you can call me Ernie. This beautiful doll next to me is my wife, Jeannie, and the brat next to her with two teeth missing is my daughter, Darlene."

His wife wasn't beautiful, but near enough. She had light brown hair halfway down her back and a smile that looked like the natural state of her face. She was wearing a long white robe tied in the middle by a gold cord. She held a sleeping baby in her arms. To George, she looked like pictures of the Madonna. She and her little girl, Darlene, were just regular size, regular in every way, near as he could see.

Flippo continued the introductions. "The name of the baby you see there is—" He broke off to call down to the end of the table, to Mr. Jeffers. "Hey Ralph," he said, "we decided to name this baby Dr. Pepper after one of your chimps. Do you think the chimp will mind?"

"Oh Daddy!" protested his daughter, and she buried her giggles in the white of her mother's arm. At the same time, his wife cried, "Oh Ernie!" the smile spreading, her light eyes rolling at George, inviting him to enjoy this with her.

Mr. Jeffers lifted his face from Hibbie and said, "Help yourself, Ernie. I'll fix it with the chimp."

George bobbed his head and sank down on the folding chair next to Darlene. He looked to Hibbie to see how he was taking this outlandish bunch, but his uncle's eyes were only for Mr. Jeffers. George was alone. . . . Now, if he put a brick on the damper pedal of his piano, so that it was held down and the strings were free to vibrate, he could play the car-horn organ up close to it and hear it ring back. Yes, the strings would take up the sound, he could hear it now. Wow! Louder . . . closer . . .

"Hey! Don't you want this? You got wax in your ears!" It was the child next to him holding out a filled bowl and grinning at him.

"Thanks," he said and grinned back, pulled back.

He looked for Lolly and spotted her leaning against the van, her arms crossed, looking out across the grassy field. Suddenly she sprinted away towards a tall woman who was wearing a long dark cape, like Dracula.

Mrs. Jeffers turned her head to see who was coming and

cried, "Come along, Miss Wilma. You're just in time. Have you seen Edgar?" She could be heard clear back to Mullin's Lake.

There was no answer from the woman, who strode smoothly, as if floating, holding Lolly's hand in hers, bending her head to the girl.

At first, George had the impression she was wearing some kind of mask, an African one perhaps, like a painted witch doctor. Up close, he saw the tattoos.

She stood next to Mrs. Jeffers, an imposing, strange figure, while Lolly made the introductions. To George and Hibbie, Lolly said, "This is Miss Wilma Pugmire," as if introducing them to a queen. Miss Wilma Pugmire stood as tall as Hibbie.

She inclined her head regally and reached out to shake George's hand as if bestowing a favor. Her cape fell back, and he saw an arm like a magazine: a glimpse of dragons, of landscapes, of wreathed cherubs. He longed to stare, to read her like a book.

Around the table, Miss Wilma was being greeted. Everyone called her Miss Wilma as if without the *Miss* it would be too intimate, too presumptuous. Her black hair, held in place by a large Spanish comb, was threaded with gray and twisted to the top of her head. She looked down at everyone through gold-rimmed glasses, for all the world like Miss Duffy, George's homeroom teacher. Same long bony face, plain flat cheeks with deep grooves to the thin lips. But the resemblance stopped there. This one was in glorious Technicolor, tattoos everywhere, face, hands, everywhere he could see. He didn't know what to do with his eyes. They wanted to be everywhere at once, take her all in, go in and under that cape and eyeball every inch.

With immense dignity, Miss Wilma took the seat next to George. To Mrs. Jeffers, she said, "What is it you asked me, Marjorie dear?"

"Have you seen Edgar? He's invited."

"He'll be along. He says for everyone to go ahead. He's waiting for his phone call from Mildred."

"That daughter of his is like clockwork," said Jeannie, in the act of pouring catsup over her husband's chili. He had a napkin tucked under his chin like a high-chair kid. "Every Friday without fail," she said to her husband.

"Sure, hon," he agreed, "you're absolutely right. She's a good girl."

Lolly handed Miss Wilma a bowl of chili as if placing it on an altar.

"Thank you, Eula dear," said the Tattooed Lady. She smiled, showing long gray teeth. She touched Lolly's hibiscus flower with a sure finger. "The swelling is down, and I see it took nicely. Have you forgiven her yet, Ralph?" She asked this of Mr. Jeffers, turning her head to him slowly.

He scowled at her and said, "Never!" Fixing on Lolly, he said, "One more like that, and I send you back home to your aunt in Florida. I mean that, Lolly."

George followed this exchange in confusion. Why would she want to lie about that, too?

Lolly cried, "You send me back, and I'll kill myself, I swear!"

Her mother looked up from feeding the chimp and flashed, "Stop that! Threats. That's all it is, empty threats. The last time we had to have the police out. And where were you? Cozy as can be, back in Okra's cage! 'You'll never see me again,' she writes, and there she is curled up safe and sound, just to drive us crazy.

" 'Kid doesn't write a note like this for nothin',' said that red-faced policeman. Well, I told him good! 'We're workin' people,' I said. 'We got no time for such shenanigans!' I said." Mrs. Jeffers was a good mimic and imitated her characters with deep relish.

Mr. Jeffers went doggedly on. "No more. I'm warning you. Of all the damn fool things to do. Tattoos! Beggin' your pardon, Miss Wilma."

"No, no, I quite agree. I thank my lucky stars my first husband was a real artist. But if I hadn't been such a green girl when I started, I wouldn't have done it."

She addressed the table at large, commanding attention. "I was fourteen years of age, just about as old as Lolly here. I was just a farm girl in Mount Pales, Kansas, when the carnival hit town, and I was told that I could see the world if I were tattooed. So I let him do it, my husband-to-be that is, and we left together and I did see the world."

Flippo's rich laugh interrupted. "And the world saw you, Miss Wilma."

Calmly she said, "Yes, you might say that, Ernie." She leaned across George to pinch Darlene's cheek. "Sweet thing," she said.

To Lolly, who sat opposite her, she said, "You're not an ignorant girl like I was, Eula dear. Body painting isn't for everyone," she said with satisfaction. She untied the cape at the neck and threw it back across the chair as if unveiling a museum piece.

George felt like applauding.

Lolly leaned across the table to her and breathed, "People just have to look at you to admire you, Miss Wilma. It's all there for them to see. You don't have to *do* anything, you don't have to *be* anything. It's just all there. You're somebody. And that's why I thought *I* would, you know." She touched her arm where the flower bloomed. "Oh, I can't explain!"

"No explanation necessary," rasped her mother. "I understand perfectly well, and if you think paintin' yourself up is goin' to do it, then you might as well. Not much else there that I can see," she added bluntly. She pulled Joey from her shoulder to kiss the top of his head, not taking her eyes from her daughter.

"I tell you, I won't have it!" rapped Mr. Jeffers from the other end.

Just then a man appeared at the table. He was wearing a brown fedora and a white shirt open at the neck, the sleeves neatly buttoned at the wrists. George looked down the table to Hibbie for help. What jumped to his mind were the monster nightmares of his childhood, his uncle always there to chase them away. NO! shouted his mind.

Chapter 6

Mr. Jeffers rose and went to the man. "Edgar, these are our new friends, George Weiss and Hibbert Whipple. Lolly there found 'em. Boys, you are lookin' at the famous, the one and only, Mr. Ugly. That's the name for all the marks out there. To us, he's Mr. Edgar Dawes, in person." He clapped the man across the twisted shoulders and returned to his seat.

Edgar Dawes removed the hat and sat down across from George. Without the hat, the bulge that pulled the eye could be seen as a spongy mass of gray folds like a naked brain. A similar cluster on the opposite jaw pulled the mouth and clung to the ear like limpets. One soft brown eye regarded George and then turned to Hibbie.

"Pleased to meet you, I'm sure." The voice was wispy and choked, as if it were being pushed through too small a space.

"Did you get your call, Edgar?" Jeannie wanted to know.

Miss Wilma said, "How is the dear girl? Has she felt life yet?"

"Yes indeed I did, Jeannie, thank you. She's fine, Miss Wilma. Sends her regards. The baby moved Wednesday morning right when she was doing the breakfast dishes, she says. She screamed aloud, and poor Jim left the pumps and came running in a fright." He paused to stare at his spoon as if a face were there. "More and more she reminds me of her mother, God rest her. Like a bulldog she was, once she had an idea. Same with Mildred. Never stops. After me all the time to come down there with them." He shook his head and then paid attention to his chili.

George didn't watch the feeding.

"Well, why the hell not, Edgar?" Mr. Jeffers wiped his mouth with a quick hand and put his spoon down. "Why not let Mildred and Jim take care of you for a change? You've earned it. Ain't you ready to take it easy?"

Flippo, in a poor imitation of W. C. Fields, said, "What? And leave show biz?"

Marjorie Jeffers reached for his empty bowl and as she refilled it said, "I bet that Mrs. McCormack, the crackpot who writes for the newspaper in this here town of whatcha-macallit, would be glad to see you go. Did you all see that complaint about us in the paper yesterday? Wrote a whole half column about us, she did. She'd close down every ten-in-one in the country if she could, that one. The old busybody. She says, 'Ooooh, how cruuuelll to make a display of human nature gone haywire.' Her very words. Calls the ten-in-ones shameful for makin' money off of 'nature's mistakes' as she calls 'em. What do you think, Joey?" she asked the baby chimp.

Lolly answered George's unspoken question. "Ten-in-ones are freak shows." She said it without emotion and then lowered her eyes once again to her bowl. She hadn't lifted her spoon.

Mr. Edgar Dawes's hobbled voice barely reached down the table. "She's not saying anything new, Marjorie. People have been saying that for ages."

"Yeah, some people don't think it's nice to stare," chuckled Mr. Jeffers.

Mr. Ugly seemed to smile. "What she doesn't know is that we stare back double. Isn't that so, Miss Wilma? Ernie? We stare at one another, them and us, and sometimes we wonder as we see what's what out there. I think of us as a bunch of exiles, staring at the shore. Wouldn't you say?" He looked around the table, taking them all in, polite and yet somehow entirely isolated. George heard his voice as the solo notes of wheezy bellows. "As for retiring," he continued, "I say feetfirst I'll retire. I owe carny life everything. I'll tell you one thing, it purely saved me. It saved me from a life locked in some back room in my parents' house, may God forgive them. They didn't know what in the world to do except hide me."

"There's many of our friends saved from a cellar life by the carny," said Flippo. "And many poor devils still in 'em. Not me. A good family makes all the difference. I had a fine family back in South Dakota, brothers and sisters to boot, all making me feel good as anyone. But I was lucky and I know it. Just wanted to be independent. Thanks to the traveling life, I got a good bit put by. . . . Couple of years more, mebbe we'll be ready to buy a little something back in Pierre and see if my folks can put up with my wife here. Whaddaya say, Jeannie?"

"It's not good for people to feel alone in affliction," persisted Mr. Ugly. "It drives them inward. Makes them ugly."

This spread a smile around the table. Mr. Dawes stood up and tipped his hat as if hearing applause. He leaned over to Lolly and in a courtly way said, "Not that you know a thing in the world about ugly, Lolly dear."

George looked quickly to see if Hibbie had been listening. "Alone in affliction," Mr. Dawes had said. All the nights of his life he could see his uncle reading the paper, rocking in his chair, watching TV, going to his room. "Good night all" was what he always said before the door closed. Did he stutter when he said that? George couldn't remember, and yet *alone in affliction* made his eyes sting. Was that what it was for Hibbie? But he's got *me*, thought George wildly.

Hibbie's big body pressed against the table as he blurted, "W-w-what if they laugh?" His intensity reached out to everyone.

"Laugh right back!" said Flippo promptly. "Like Edgar here said, if they stare, stare back double. If they laugh, laugh back more'n they give."

Mr. Jeffers' answer was to wave a scornful hand. "So what?"

His wife took up the theme. "Pay 'em no mind, honey. They're only dopes. Who cares?" She shrugged a careless shoulder.

Miss Wilma had an announcement. "Stupidity laughs." She lifted her royal head to warn Lolly, "Never be stupid, my child."

Lolly, as if given a holy charge, said solemnly, "No, Miss Wilma."

Mr. Ugly turned his ponderous head to Hibbie. "That kind of laughter is hard," he began and was about to say more, but George couldn't wait.

"If you stay away from people, you don't get laughed at."

Mr. Dawes nodded his head up and down as he gave this his attention. "Certainly. I wasn't laughed at when I was locked away in the back room of my parents' house. Is that what you mean?"

Just then, Mr. Jeffers rose from his chair to cup an ear to the shouts of a man striding across the field towards them. The man, seeing that he had Mr. Jeffers' attention, stopped where he was and waved the whip in his hand for Mr. Jeffers to come to him.

"Trouble!" shouted the man. He was dressed in riding breeches, and he slapped at them as he called, "The new Bozo. A fight. Come on, Ralph. Hurry up."

"Be right there, Wallen," shouted Mr. Jeffers and said to the table, "Sorry, folks." He looked at Hibbie as if weighing him. "Want to come, young fella? We may need an arm."

George wasn't about to be left behind. He jumped up and so did Lolly, both following in the wake of Mr. Jeffers and Hibbie. "What's a Bozo?" he asked her.

"Pooh. Who doesn't know a Bozo? Fresh mouth, that's what. Like you. You'll see."

Chapter 7

At the far end of the midway, a noisy crowd had gathered in front of a booth that had above it a brightly lit fluorescent sign: DROP THE BOZO. Mr. Jeffers, Hibbie and the man in the riding breeches shouldered their way through the buzzing, jostling people to the very front of the booth. George and Lolly were close behind.

Two angry men in overalls were hurling baseballs at a small figure perched on a narrow board six feet above a large tank of water. At either end of his seat were levers, and above those were two small circles, bull's-eyes for the throwers to aim at. The face of the seated man was painted like a clown's, although the rest of him was ordinary enough—

tan work pants and T-shirt both dripping wet. He was taunting the furious men in a particularly nasty way, a voice of nasal nastiness that scraped George's nerves. "Yah, you couldn't hit the side of a barn with your pillow, ya fat slobs!" The men were not aiming for the targets. What they wanted was to hit the white face, black eyes, red nose directly. They wanted to still that awful red mouth for good and all. George grabbed at Lolly in alarm. There was murder in the air! If it weren't for the chicken wire strung in front of that poor mutt up there, he'd be a goner! The crowd egged on the two men, taking sides, the exasperated pitchers the odds-on favorites. With both hands, the men scooped up the balls from a bin, ignoring the woman pleading with them to pay up or stop. They threw to maim. By chance, one of the balls hit the small circle at the end of the plank. The board broke away and dumped the Bozo into the tank of water. The crowd cheered. The Bozo emerged and climbed up to his perch again. "Dumb luck," he jeered. "Are your wives as dumb as you?"

At this, one of the men threw a leg over the booth. He was going to get the Bozo if it was the last thing he did. Mr. Jeffers sprang forward and put a restraining hand on the leg. The other man, seeing his friend stopped, at last had an outlet for his anger right at hand. He was ready to sock a brick wall. Mr. Jeffers would be better than a wall. The man grabbed Lolly's father to spin him around and raised a fist.

The crowd surged forward. Oh, boy. A fight! Action!

At this, Wallen faced the crowd and with hands raised in surrender urged them not to push closer. "Okay, folks, give us room. Everything's under control here. Stay back, please."

He looked over his shoulder in time to see Hibbie grab

the upraised arm of the man who was about to clobber Mr. Jeffers. He held the arm up like a prize. No effort, just held it up. Everyone stopped for a moment in surprise, even the struggling man who owned the arm. It was as if someone had yelled "FREEZE!" Mr. Jeffers used this moment to say a few quiet words to the man about to lunge over the booth. With a sheepish nod, the leg was withdrawn. Hibbie looked down at the red face of his catch and smiled his wide apologetic smile. He released him.

Mr. Wallen again addressed the crowd. "It's all over, folks. Wallen's Carnival provides another free show. There's more to be seen down at the Cooch Tent. Girls, girls, girls, like you've never seen before! The show is about to begin!"

This broke up the crowd like an ice jam. Mr. Wallen peeled off a bill and handed it to the two men who were standing by, suddenly aware that they were onstage, and looking somewhat pleased with themselves. "Here, you go see the show. The treat's on me." The blond man stuffed the bill in a pocket and jerked his head toward the Bozo, still huddled on the plank. "He sure goaded me, mister. He sure made me mad. He says that again about my wife, and I'll get him for sure." Mr. Wallen just nodded.

As they ambled away, he called out to the Bozo, "Hey, you! Come down here!"

Under the paint, George saw a high school kid not so much older than he, a long wisp of a boy who looked scared and chilled.

"You're not the regular Bozo. Where is he? Never mind, you're fired." The Carnival owner slapped his crop against his boots as if aching to use it elsewhere.

"Aw, Mr. Wallen, I was just doing my job. I'm the supper replacement, just learning. This is just my second day."

"Well it's your last. You're supposed to insult the mark so he parts with his money, but keep the crowd on *your* side. You realize that bunch of people just now were ready to see you killed? You're no Bozo, son. If it weren't for this man here, and him"—he motioned to Hibbie and Mr. Jeffers standing behind him—"you'd have been torn apart by those rubes. You got to walk a thin line, and it's not easy. The rule is, insult them but make them laugh—not mad. You're no Bozo and never will be. Get your things and get out of here. We'll close the Bozo until the regular comes on tonight."

Lolly at once cried, "Hey, let me be the Bozo tonight, Uncle Larry. I can do it. I know I can! I'd be a good one!" Neither of the older men paid the slightest attention. She might as well have been a fly buzzing around.

She turned to George, who at that moment was looking around trying to locate the source of a high-pitched hum he was hearing that bothered him. It must be from the fluorescent lights up there, he decided. It must be from the Bozo sign. He hadn't heard a word of what Lolly said, and had no idea what she was talking about when she said, "I would, too! Don't you think? They don't even listen to me!"

It was Hibbie whose gray green eyes showed he not only listened but heard her. "I know how you f-f-feel," he said, putting his big solid hand to her shoulder. Again she had no chance to talk it out, because just then Hibbie's attention was drawn away by Mr. Wallen.

"Thanks, mister," said the Carnival owner to Hibbie, taking his hand and pumping it. "Wouldn't have gotten off so easy tonight if you hadn't been around. Ralph here is getting all wracked up wrestling his gorilla. Pretty soon we'll have to find a nice soft cage to put him in himself. Ain't that so, Ralph?"

"Not far off, Larry. There's life in the old boy yet, but flickerin', flickerin'. I need a new arm like Hibbie here."

"Where you from, son?" the owner asked him. "You work around here?"

A direct question. Very tough for Hibbie. He threw George an agonized glance, and the boy was about to answer for him when Lolly spoke up. "He's a Dugan Man, Uncle Larry. He drives a truck around Mullin's Bridge and delivers stuff like bread and cake."

"Well now, look who answers when she's not spoken to," said Mr. Wallen, eyes hidden by dark glasses, but temper in the curl of the lips. "Right now I'm talking to this young fella."

Hibbie was off the hook and didn't have to speak up, but to George's vast surprise, he did. "She w-w-was only doing me a fa . . ." And then poor old Unc got himself into one of the awful blocks he couldn't get out of. Like some living thing had him by his insides and was shaking the daylights out of him. He couldn't let go, couldn't let go of the word that started it. His eyes bulged and his mouth twisted and his belly heaved and nobody knew where to look. Anywhere but at him.

Just then the lights strung all along the midway lit up. It was as if the whole Carnival had sprung to life, and that broke it for Hibbie. He stopped. George could have kissed every light bulb.

Everybody moved at once. Mr. Wallen, with a nod to all, turned on his heel as soon as the lights went on. Lolly's father took Hibbie by the elbow and steered him away. "C'mon, kids," said Mr. Jeffers. They headed across the field. "Jeffers Jungle's gotta open tonight."

The dinner guests had gone, the table had been cleared

and put away as if no one had been there. People were strolling around the canvas-covered ring examining what they could see of the setup, waiting for it to open. A line had formed to buy tickets from Lolly's mother, who sat at a bridge table in front of the flap. She looked up as they neared.

"Shake a leg there. I almost had a posse out for you. Get on up here, Ralph. The mike is on and waitin'."

Ralph Jeffers sprang up to the platform, grabbed the mike and started talking in one fluid motion.

"Step right up, ladies and gentlemen, you are about to see the most unique, the most unusual, the one and only show of its kind in the entire world. It's called Jeffers Jungle. Ever hear of it? Of course you have. And why not? Kings have. Presidents have. Monarchs and emperors of vast countries have heard of Jeffers Jungle, so it's fair to say that you have too. We are the Wrestlin' Chimps. Fair game for any red-blooded American to take on and get the surprise of his life. A show you'll not forget, nor your sweetie neither. Now let me show you what I mean. Okra, come out here, honey."

He ducked inside the van for a moment and returned leading the little chimp by the hand. Okra was a real ham and blew kisses to the audience.

From down below, the chimp looked even lighter and smaller than in the cage. Betcha Uncle Hib could take her easy, thought George. He whispered to his uncle, "Can'tcha, Hib?"

"What?"

"You can take that chimp easy, don't you think?"

"All these people, George. That's what I'm thinking of."

"Then just think of the five bucks."

A big laugh from the crowd drew their attention. They saw that Okra had climbed up to Jeffers' arms and was carefully examining his hair, sniffing her fingers after touching.

"Your chimp finding her dinner?" yelled a voice.

"Don't be fooled by size, ladies and gentlemen," said Mr. Jeffers. "Okra here is no pushover. You'll see a good fight for your money, not countin' my own battle with the most ferocious gorilla captured by man. Whoever goes into the ring with my girl here will wear a helmet and face guard, while Okra here will go muzzled and wear gloves. That right, Okra?"

The chimp pursed her lips and nuzzled his ear. Then getting down to business, Mr. Jeffers set the chimp down on her feet and called out, "Okay, now who out there is ready to step in the ring for a go-around with this chimp? Five dollars in your pocket if you pin both shoulders to the mat, and fifty cents more for each second you keep 'em there. Come on, any strappin' fella out there ready to show us what he can do?"

A voice from the crowd called out, "How much do that there animal weigh, mister? Not more'n ten pounds soaking wet is my bet. So what's the fight?"

"Eighty-three pounds by scale this very mornin', sir. Less than the little lady standin' by your side. Care to take on my chimp?"

All eyes swiveled to the heckler and were disappointed to see a small man, old and bent, not likely to be wrestling a chimpanzee.

Mr. Jeffers scanned the audience and then looked down at Hibbie. Pretending surprise, he said, "Aha! I see a perfect physical specimen right under my nose. How about you, sir? Care to wrestle my chimp?"

Despite the smallness of the animal, George felt a warning hollow in the pit of his stomach when his uncle nodded. It suddenly seemed like such a damn fool thing to do—wrestle a chimp and maybe get bitten or rabies or something.

Mr. Jeffers leaned over the platform with hand outstretched to give Hibbie a lift up. A small commotion in the rear made him look up.

Various voices cried out, "Here he is, mister."

"Back here is who you want."

"Go on, Charlie. Charlie will do it!"

Mr. Jeffers shaded his eyes to see back there. "Sure. Come on up, Charlie, wherever you are. The more the merrier."

A big, beer-bellied man was shoved through the crowd by his giggling companions, two women carrying stuffed animals and a small wiry man in a sailor hat, all three pretending to be working very hard moving Charlie along. The big man, his shirttails hanging and his tie knot under his ear, was laughing and protesting, but he let himself be hauled to the front and then to the platform.

Hibbie and Charlie stood sheepishly side by side, making the small black creature they were about to wrestle seem even smaller. George felt sweaty with embarrassment seeing his uncle up there.

"No fair!" cried someone in the crowd.

Mr. Jeffers seemed to be expecting this. He said, "Okay then, tell you what I'm gonna do. I'll give you boys a choice if you think the chimp is too easy. Okra here may not be the one for you. Give me one more second of your time."

Once again he darted inside the van and emerged, this time with Li'l Sis. The crowd drew breath as one person, a gasp of pure primitive awe at the sight of the gorilla. Li'l

Sis haunched down beside Mr. Jeffers and regarded the mass of people before him with indifferent eyes.

"Now here you have frisky Okra, ready and willin' to take you on, or, if you prefer, Li'l Sis here will oblige. You have a choice gentlemen, who will it be? Okra, step up." He held out something to her, she ate it and stepped forward to bow to the two men.

"Now let's hear from you, Li'l Sis." He patted the gorilla once, and immediately the animal sprang to life. He stood, thumped his chest and let loose a roar so ferocious that George's teeth rattled in his head. A wind of fear and tension passed over the audience, causing eyes to glitter and here and there an eruption of nervous giggles.

"Now who will it be, my friends? My chimp or my gorilla?"

Neither man was able to speak. No one in the crowd dared heckle. The gorilla wasn't even leashed.

"Well then, I'll choose for you. I'll make it easy for you. *You* fight the chimp, and *I'll* fight the gorilla. How's that for fair?"

Mr. Jeffers clapped his hands together smartly. "All right, folks, we have a spectacle! Line up right here for your tickets, and we'll see you inside. You boys come with me."

Chapter 8

While Mr. Jeffers made his pitch outside on the platform, Lolly and her mother set up the bleachers inside the tent. Although there was room for more than a hundred people, it was soon packed.

Lolly found her way to George. He was sitting near the front staring up at Hibbie, who was already in the ring with Charlie and Mr. Jeffers.

"Hi," she said, "how do you like it so far? You hear my father out there? Isn't he something? Where's Hibbie?"

George could have listened to that wonderful voice ask questions all night. His only answer was to gesture with a thumb to the ring.

She hadn't noticed him up there. It was the first she knew about Hibbie wrestling in the show.

"The chimp?" she gasped. And when George nodded, she grabbed his shirt as if she just had news of an accident. "Don't let him do it. No. Really. Don't let him do it. He doesn't know what he's getting into. Don't do it, Hibbie," she shrilled up to him.

Mr. Jeffers heard this and lifted his eyes to her with a blaze that would have stopped a charging bull. He simply pointed an index finger, and she subsided on the bench. Unc must have heard too, because he looked down and smiled and shrugged.

George was all at sea. She acts like it's the end of the world, like one of those TV actresses on the soaps who has just heard that her trench mouth is spreading all over her body. Look at that chest on him. What could a little chimp do to him after all? Why does she have to be so dramatic about everything?

In full view of the crowd, Charlie and Hibbie drew straws to see who would fight Okra first. Big-bellied Charlie pulled the short one. He would fight first.

Lolly sighed "Good" into George's ear, and he said "What?" so she would do it again.

Charlie was in the spirit of the thing now and held up the straw for all to see, strutting around the ring like a winner. He had taken off his shirt and tie and just had on his short-sleeved undershirt. George remembered him suddenly. He had seen him in the firehouse at Mullin's Bridge sometimes, playing cards with other firemen or polishing the engine, a beefy red-faced man tending to business. He could hardly recognize the grinning loose-lipped man in the stained undershirt, showing off for his friends, shadowboxing around the ring, acting like he's the whole show. He pretended to jab at Hibbie, who just stood there looking down at his shoes, an embarrassed grin on his face. George wanted to sweep him up and take him home, get them both out of there. He looked around as if awakening. What were they doing there? The noise and the blood excitement of the crowd made him feel pushed, as if he needed more air.

Mr. Jeffers told Hibbie to wait in the bleachers. "Won't take long, son," he said, with a wink at Charlie.

"And don't I know it," Charlie announced to the crowd. "Who's he going to fight?" He slapped his chest and yelled like Tarzan swinging on a vine.

Hibbie jumped down from the ring and squeezed in between George and Lolly.

"Let's go home," whispered George.

"Can't."

"Why not?"

"Wouldn't be right."

Charlie's friends were on the other side of the ring cheering him on. "You tell 'em, Charlie honey." "Atta way, Charlie!"

Mr. Jeffers handed him a helmet and face guard like baseball catchers wear. "Here, put these on."

At first Charlie didn't want to, but Mr. Jeffers insisted. There was something about Mr. Jeffers' sudden seriousness that sobered the fat man somewhat.

Then Mr. Jeffers brought out Okra, and the crowd went wild. Around her middle, she had on a ballet tutu that once upon a time was pink. A muzzle and gloves were put on her. She was led to a corner, where she sat and scratched.

Charlie was asked to go to the other corner, and Mr. Jeffers announced as if for a heavyweight crown, "In this corner, we have the defender, name of Okra. A real swinger folks. Of trees, heh, heh. Weight: 83 pounds. Height: 3 feet. Arm reach: around the corner."

He held up Okra's arm for applause.

"In the other corner, we have the challenger, Mr. Charlie Stamp, of that great metropolis Mullin's Bridge. Fireman, I think you said, sir? Will his fire be put out tonight? That is the question. Five dollars in his pocket for only two minutes of his time engaged in fair fight and still with us or for pinnin' Okra's dainty shoulders to the mat. Come on over here, Charlie. Let's see you."

The crowd whistled and razzed as the man bunched his muscles, turning and posing this way and that like Mr. America.

"Okay then, let's go!" Mr. Jeffers slapped a bell.

Charlie danced out. Behind the mask, the big grin was still in place, fists at the ready.

Okra had dozed off.

Charlie bounced over to her and shouted, "Hey!" When the chimp didn't move, he stood over her with his hands on his hips, puzzled. What to do? He looked around for Mr. Jeffers.

"Want me to wake her up for you?" Mr. Jeffers asked mildly. He picked up the chimp, shook her a bit and set her down again with a pat on her behind. She waddled around on her bandy legs, scarcely awake. Then she noticed Charlie, and suddenly she sprang to his shoulder. She put her arms around him like a lover.

"She your wife?" yelled a voice.

"Want us to turn out the lights?" yelled another.

But the mood of the crowd shifted suddenly. The good humor was gone, and people began shouting for their money back. They knew it. There was no fight. What a gyp!

Charlie made a move. Okra had left him and was waddling away, not interested anymore. He put his hand on her arm to get her attention.

He got it.

The force of her lunge knocked him to the mat. Her arms swept from top to bottom in one black blur of motion. Not even a breath between one moment and the next, just one turbulent wave faster than the eye could follow. It was as if seen through a speeded-up camera. Man up, man down, a streak of black arms, and it was all over in nothing flat. Charlie lay on the mat like a beached whale, his mask gone, his clothes in ribbons, gasping for air.

While everyone was trying to take in what had happened, Okra straddled him, pulled off his shoe and sock and rubbed the sole of his foot with her nose.

Charlie wasn't ticklish at that moment.

Mr. Jeffers removed Okra and helped Charlie to his feet. Now everyone was for the dazed man. He tried to pull what was left of his clothing around him to hide the boxer shorts. He waved weakly to the crowd to show he was okay and limped off.

Now that the audience knew what to expect, they were eager for the next fight.

"You can't do it, Hib," cried George, now thoroughly alarmed for his uncle. Okra's punches were still vibrating in his head like gongs. He wasn't going to let Hib do that, get punched out with everyone laughing. Hadn't he had enough of that kind of laughing? He looked at Lolly angrily, then realized she did try to stop it. But still . . . they had done her a good turn, picked her up, brought her back here and now look. Hib was going to get hurt.

He stood up and pulled on Hibbie's arm to do the same. "Come on, Unc. We're going home." Hibbie didn't budge.

"I can't do that, George. I told you befff . . . I already told you. I said to Mr. Jeffers that I would, and I can't go back on that. He expects me."

He sat there shaking his head, the dumb ox, staring straight ahead. Stubborn as a rock, once he got hold of something he thought was right. There was no moving him. If only George were bigger, stronger, quicker, smarter, he would be able to protect his uncle. Would be able to change his mind, make him see.

Lolly also stood. She stamped her foot and said, "Get out of here, Hibbie, like George says. I would never in a million years have brought you home with me if I thought I'd get you into this!" She was suddenly into something, a genuine moan escaping her. "Oh God, it's all my fault! Isn't that just like me? Everything I do turns wrong!"

She was taking it all on herself, and that wasn't helping anything. "Never mind *you*!" George hissed at her, "What are we going to do about *him*? He'll never leave, I'm telling you!"

"Well think of something then!" cried Lolly, both of them flinging their jitters at one another above Hibbie's head, like battling parents.

Then George did think of something. He doubled over, crying loudly, "Oh God, the pain!"

This got Hibbie to his feet. "Hey, what's the matter with you?"

"I don't know," gasped the afflicted boy, sinking to his

knees. "I have the most awful pain. Right here. I think I'm going to throw up."

Lolly got it. "Air!" she commanded. "He needs air! Hibbie, let's get him outside. Make way there."

The people around them witnessed George's agony and were helpful.

"Don't let him puke on me!"

"My Aunt Minna died with a pain like that."

"Hey, what did you do to the kid?"

"Looks too late for a doctor to me."

Hibbie lifted George in his arms like a baby and pushed his way through the crowd to the exit. Mr. Jeffers caught up with them. "Where ya goin'? You're on next! What's the matter with him?"

"Where's a doctor, Mr. Jeffers? George is sick or something. He's in terrible pain. Quick, you have a doctor around here?"

"Lolly, take 'em to Dr. Bilder over in the first-aid tent, you know where that is." He put his hand on George's forehead, drooped on Hibbie's breast as if in a coma. "No fever that I can feel. Oh well, look, I've got to get back, see if there's anyone else I can hustle. Sorry about this, son. You'd be a good contender."

"I wouldn't do this to you for anything, Mr. Jeffers. I'm real ssssorry to disappoint you. But it's George."

"Go on, take 'em, Lolly." He waved them off across the field to the bright lights of the midway.

When they reached the midway, George said, "Okay, Uncle Hib. You can put me down now."

Chapter 9

Hib nearly dropped him. First he was incredulous, then furious, then relieved, each emotion hanging out a sign on his artless face. Finally he laughed and roughed George's hair. "You're s-s-some actor, know that, kid? You sure had me fooled." To Lolly, he said, "You cook this up with him?" In the cheer of the moment, all three of them standing around in the lights of the midway, grinning at one another, George realized suddenly that he had never seen his uncle so free and easy with someone outside the family before.

"Just helped," said Lolly, her delicate face lit with humor. "Genius here had the brainstorm. For a second there, George, you really had me going too. But then I caught on.

I was just mama's little helper." That last sentence struck her and she repeated it ruefully. "Yeah, mama's little helper."

"Do we go home now or what?" asked George. "We sure aren't going to go back there!" motioning to Jeffers Jungle.

Hibbie looked off above their heads down the midway as if hearing the angels call. "Just one thing I want to see first, okay, George? Just ffffive minutes. Let's go back to the Bozo."

What did he want to do that for? Usually Hib loved the pinball machines in the Arcade. How queer everything was. Everything was going to be so great this morning. And now it was like some dream he was having. Mom leaves and they have this job together, and instead of doing all their *things* like always—eating out of cans, working on his great new invention, nothing much to say and no one to bother them, just comfortable like always—what happens? First thing you know, they're traipsing around a carnival, buddying up with a tattooed girl. Was it just this morning they met her? Seems like years ago.

They could hear the mocking nasty voice on the night air before they came to it. The Bozo was doing a good business, a big crowd around the booth watching him get his ducking. He was painted up with the same kind of clown face as the earlier Bozo, but this one had the crowd laughing instead of angry.

A neatly dressed man stepped up to the booth to take out a billfold and handed some money to the cashier. She reached into the barrel by her side and lined up a dozen balls on the ledge in front of him. He slowly removed his jacket and handed it to the white-haired lady next to him. She folded it carefully over her arm and bowed her head as if telling him he could now begin. He passed a hand over his slicked-back hair, which together with his long narrow face and pencil-thin mustache made him seem like a department store dummy in action. He picked up a ball and hefted it. The Bozo said, "Aren't you going to take off the vest? Probably full of holes under there, folks."

The man ignored this and threw the ball at the target. It fell short. The crowd laughed, but he didn't crack a smile. The Bozo jeered, "Take it off, take it off! Might muss your pretty shirtums and Mama might spank." The man said seriously, "You're right," but instead of taking off the vest, he rolled up his sleeves.

Several more balls went wild. "Let the lady throw, you pen pusher. Bet she can do better than you any day." The man was concentrated with a single purpose. He continued to throw balls until one of them finally reached the target. He struck the bull's-eye, and the Bozo was abruptly dumped. The man nodded his head, completely satisfied, even though there was a ball still left on the ledge to throw. He unrolled his sleeves as carefully as before, held out his hand for his jacket, and when it was on, smoothed and buttoned, he gave his arm to the lady and they went off in the night, leaving the ball on the ledge like a tip.

By the time the Bozo had climbed out of the water and was sitting once again on his perch, he had chosen his next victim. It was Hibbie, up front and not to be missed. His shaggy head rose above the crowd; much below on either side of him were George and Lolly.

"Aha. I see the baby boy is out tonight with his mommy and daddy," rasped the Bozo. "Hey, you there with the big ears. Can you toss overhand yet?"

Hibbie looked around with the others to see who the Bozo

was teasing, and when he realized it was himself, he chortled and flushed and wagged his head as if it were the funniest thing he ever heard.

Lolly leaned over the ledge to call up to the Bozo, "Cut it out, Wilson. He's with me!"

The Bozo peered out and in his real voice, he said, "Oh, that you, Lolly? Didn't see you. Hold it. Be right there. I want to talk to you." He yelled to the audience, "Bozo is closing down for five minutes, folks. Even the Bozo gotta go. Be back with you soon, you suckers. Stick around."

Lolly led George and Hibbie around the side to wait for him.

A gangling young man with a wide friendly smile shook hands with them. Wilson put a damp arm around Lolly. "I haven't seen you since the artwork. Here, let's have a look at it."

Wilson examined Lolly's arm, touching it carefully, regarding the tropical flower as if looking at stretched canvas. "Mmmmm, looks good to me. Real good. Nice texture. I hear tell your old man nearly bit your head off. That so? You tell him who did it?"

"You know I wouldn't do any such thing. Didn't I say I wouldn't? Besides, pooh, he didn't mind a bit."

Wilson was skeptical. "Not the way I heard it. Way I heard it, his gorilla would be gnawing my bones if he knew it was me."

Lolly ignored this. "So now that it's okay, when can you do another one? I know just what I want this time! I want my sign. A big Libra, across here."

Across her chest! Across her . . . George shot Hibbie a glance to see if he had heard. Maybe he could understand what was going on. Where's her sense?

70

Wilson said, "That's why I wanted to see you, Lolly." He glanced around hurriedly to see if anyone else was listening and then lowered his voice as if he were about to tell her where the loot was stashed. "I'm leaving," he said. "Leaving the Carny end of next week."

Lolly was aghast and burst into hot tears. As if it were a personal insult, a strike against her alone, she cried, "Why are you doing this to me? What for? I thought you wanted to do me. 'Be my masterpiece,' you said. I'll kill myself if you go! You said I'd be somebody when we were all done."

"You said that, Lolly. I didn't." Wilson was firm about that. "Hey, what's the matter with you? What's such a big deal?" He held the wrist that wiped the tears and shook it gently for attention. "Don't talk like that, Lolly. Don't be silly. You're not going to kill yourself. You talked me into one tattoo, but that's as far as I go. Look. I have a chance to go to art school in Philly. A real art school. My uncle says he'll pay, and I'm going. It's a big chance for me. The semester starts week after next, and I'm going to be there. You guys can understand that!"

"You tell Mr. Wallen yet?" asked the mournful voice.

Wilson's confident manner collapsed. "No. He's going to be plenty sore at me I know. He trained me himself, and I hate to disappoint him. I'll tell him, don't worry. I have to get my nerve up first. Or somehow find a replacement."

Suddenly Lolly surprised them all by a jet of laughter while the tears were still fresh. "I told Uncle Larry I wanted to be the new Bozo, but he didn't even listen to me. But now he won't have anybody, so here's my chance. How about me, Wilson? I've watched you enough, I don't even need the training. I'll be the new Bozo!"

"Sure. And I'm the new Rembrandt."

"No, I mean it. Why not?"

Wilson still kept the teasing note. "Well, for one thing, you're not nearly mean enough."

Hibbie asked quickly, "You have to be m-m-mean to be a Bozo?"

This Wilson took seriously. "Well, not really mean. I was just kidding. It may help, but . . . You really want to know this?" He broke off to look sharply at Hibbie. What he saw apparently satisfied him, for his brown eyes gleamed with interest and his long face was intent. "Yeah, well, that's what makes the job interesting. You have to know how people are. What holds them together, know what I'm saying? You size them up and use it—for or against them. For instance, a man comes up. You know he's a drinker, let's say. Well, you use that. Tell him he bends his arm hoisting so much, he can't throw a ball anymore. Or say you see someone step up with the wife, and you know he roughs her up. I can't tell you how you know, but you do. Maybe the whole town knows it, and you've mingled and picked up on this one or that. So you use that, see what I mean? Tell him he may be a tough guy at home with the wife, but let's see how tough he can be here, see if he can dump the Bozo. Also you got to use your head about what's too much. Don't want to make them too mad either. Just mad enough to part with the dough. It's hard to describe, but there's a lot more to it than people think. It's psychology." Wilson tapped his head. "I like being a Bozo, and I wouldn't give it up for anything if it weren't for this chance. . . ."

Hibbie couldn't wait for him to finish. "You think *I* c-c-could be?"

George couldn't believe his ears.

"You? A Bozo?" Wilson snorted through his nose and

then, to cover up, he asked George, "How about you? Everybody else wants to get in the act. You want to be a Bozo too?"

George dumbly shook his head no.

Wilson said to Hibbie, "You're on the heavy side. I mean you're big. We'd have to reinforce the plank, but I guess that's okay. That's not the main thing." He had to come out with it. "Look man, you stutter, right?"

He looked at Hibbie straight, and Hibbie said, "I d-d-do. But I tell you, inside I think I can do it. I want to." He tapped his barrel of a chest and laughed a short embarrassed laugh at himself.

Lolly said, "Hey, *I'm* the one. I asked first!"

Wilson bent down and kissed her forehead. "Forget it, Lolly. You think you can make the marks mad enough to dump you? They'll drool right into the water. No one is going to throw balls at a girl. Unless it's just to see you in a wet T-shirt. You want that?" He looked at Hibbie then and winked over Lolly's head. "Crazy, but cute," he said. "First she wants to be the Tattooed Lady, and now she wants to be the Bozo." In his jeering Bozo voice, he said, "What kinky adolescent have we here? A Bozo. The kid has nerve. Who does she think she is?"

Wilson didn't know Unc well enough to know those bones in his jaw only stuck out that way when he was mad.

Hib said, "She doesn't know. She doesn't know that yet."

Like she was blind, Lolly took Hibbie's hand. A deep tingle began in George's insides, and his heart gave a warning thump. He heard Wilson say "You really want the job?" and his uncle say "Yes, I do."

Then George didn't want to hear any more. He wanted to go home to his room. He knew it, he'd always known it. Once you go outside, everything gets knotted up. He and Unc used to be a team, and now look. Hanging on to Lolly's hand like it was a life preserver. Him being the Bozo when he can't even say his own name without giving people the itch.

Wilson seemed to have settled something. "Okay then. I'll take your word. Maybe you can. It will be great for me if I can tell Mr. Wallen I have a replacement already. I'll have to teach you, you understand? You come the same time tomorrow night, and if it works out, then next week we'll work together. I'll teach you all I can. I leave next Saturday, so next Saturday night, if it's okay with Wallen, you're the Bozo."

Lolly said to Hibbie, "We pull up after next week. New Paltz is next, I think."

George was incredulous. "You going to quit your job, follow the Carny, Hibbie? Leave home? Leave us? That what you're going to do?"

"I don't know," Hibbie said. "I might." He squinted as if dazed by a sudden light.

"Benedict Arnold!" George said hotly when they climbed into the car for home.

"Who?" asked Hibbie, pretending innocence. "Was he a Bozo too?"

Chapter 10

It was a gloomy, empty house they returned to, not at all what George had looked forward to that very morning. He had pictured them getting supper together, easy and fooling around, messing up like kids out of school because his mother was away. He had pictured them home, like always.

Instead, when they turned on the lights in the kitchen, George felt his mother's absence like a hole in space where the comfort of her body should be. She should be there at the old enamel table, sitting across from Hibbie over a steaming cup of tea, the drone of their voices the background music of his entire life. She should be there. She would tell Hibbie to stay put, not be pushing to change things around, not until George was more . . . what? Well, more . . . ready.

He brushed by his uncle to go upstairs, needing to leave the day behind, longing to go to his room and bury himself in his very own things, familiar and reliable and always there.

"Hey look," said Hibbie, bending over to pick up the day's mail, "a card from your grandfather." He held it up to the light as if it held a secret that would shine through. He carried it over to the kitchen table and sat down, pushing the breakfast dishes away to clear a space. He put the card down before him, as if doing homework.

George waited at the doorway.

" 'Dear Joan and Hibbert and Grandson—' " Hibbie looked up to say, "D-d-don't think he remembers your n-name there, George."

The boy thought, How do you like that? One little post-card from his father, and he can't even talk to me without his tongue getting twisted like a corkscrew.

Hibbie continued to read aloud, something he could always do smoothly.

Sally and I are fine and hope to hear the same
from you. Long time no see. Florida was 59 degrees
yesterday, too cold for me. Your stepmother and
I send our best regards.
Your father and grandfather,
Edward P. Whipple

Hibbie fell silent and looked off, his eyes unfocused as if some long-ago memory were unreeling before him. There was an expression on his face that positively enraged

George. He was raring to find an outlet for his feelings.

"What are you looking like that for? What do you care? He was glad to get rid of you! Just handed you over when Mom asked. He hit you and yelled for you to slow down. Slow down and talk right. Just a little kid. I know all that, so what do you care if he writes or not?" The spill of spite made him feel better. "Rotten old man! He gives you a whack when you open your mouth, and you care if he sends a card. You're just a patsy, a sitting duck, a Bozo all right!"

Hibbie raised a hand. "Enough," he said, tired.

It was the raised hand, that same defeated gesture he had drawn from his uncle twice already that day, that did it. Love and shame pulled George's feet a few steps towards the big man slumped at the table.

Hibbie straightened and said, "How about a little something to eat?" As he got up from the wooden chair, George saw that his words hadn't really gone deep. Wherever it was that Hibbie kept old wounds was closed to George, too far under for his reach. He hardened.

"No thanks. I'm going upstairs."

George turned and ran to his room.

As he closed his bedroom door, he leaned his back against it for a moment. He looked around his room, his haven, for the comfort it gave him just to see it.

It looked like the parts department of some very busy junk shop. Green metal office shelves climbed two of the walls. They were packed top to bottom with cartons bulging with assorted parts of forgotten machines, battered radios waiting to be fixed or taken apart, disemboweled motors, pieces of musical instruments, amplifiers, stacks of old records. The bugle hanging on the other wall he found just that past March when Mullin's Bridge had the town cleanup. He and

Hib had gotten up at dawn that day and gone around in a delighted frenzy, finding wonderful things to lug home, things just sitting out on the sidewalks, begging for them to come along and take them home before the garbage men. That was how he found the metal shelves last year. The oboe hanging up there had been his dad's; the guitar was a Christmas present from his mom and Uncle Hib. All there, all his.

Quickly he went to his closet to get the rags from the upper shelf, stacked as neatly as towels in his mom's linen closet. He carried them to the door and tucked them in all the spaces along the bottom and sides, anyplace where sound could drift through. They were his soundproofing. He didn't need them tonight. Hibbie wouldn't mind the noise, but he liked doing it just the same. It made him feel more private. Tonight he would finish the connections, and his car-horn organ would be ready to play. Might be loud. He certainly hoped so.

It had taken months to collect all the horns. They weren't as hard to find as the doorbell push buttons. Today he had had terrific luck.

What he had been planning all those months was a playable instrument made out of car horns. He had heard it in his head. He had seen it plain as day. He had pictured the car horns mounted side by side on a board, arranged in order like a scale, low to high. Each car horn was wired to a doorbell push button right in front of it. The whole thing could be played like a piano. All you had to do was press one of the buttons and, if he had wired it correctly, its own car horn would sound off. Press one after another and oh, the music he could make! A car-horn organ!

He sat at the worktable near his bed and tenderly lifted

the cloth that protected his work while he was away. For a few seconds, he sat back in his chair, worshipping. It was all before him, almost finished, more beautiful even than he had pictured it.

He frowned and bent towards it. Yes, the board that it was mounted on needed painting. Why hadn't he thought of that before he did the wiring? Maybe Con-Tact paper would do, make it look like marble. Sure, a good idea. The car horns themselves, like empty ice-cream cones stuck point down on a brownie, were as shiny as elbow grease could make them. Not all the push buttons were the same size, but he had the good idea of painting the little mounds all the same white, and the push buttons in the middle a shiny black. My little nipples, he thought, with a secret thrill. It was all ready except for one push button and then wiring it all up to the main storage battery. Last week in the dump, he had found a perfectly good charger he could use to juice up the battery when he needed to. It was all there.

He set to work, and everything dropped away from his mind but the precious parts in front of him. He bent over his work, installing the afternoon's find, his fingers nimble and knowing. His eyes were intent and concentrated. His whole body was at that moment at full attention, trained and completely there, utterly confident.

Check the leads from the car horns to the battery. Ah, beautiful. Now he could explore his instrument, he could begin to learn how to play this new addition to the great symphonies of the world. *"Ladies and gentlemen"*—like Mr. Jeffers introducing his chimps tonight—*"ladies and gentlemen, the Car-Horn Organ, invented this very century by that musical whiz, fearless George Weiss, Playboy and Hot Stuff of Mullin's Bridge. And now, Mr. President, as a little surprise for the queen here, we have asked George to play a tune in honor of her visit to our shores. He will play for her on his famous Car-Horn Organ. No, no, Queen. Don't do that. Get up—please! Don't thank me, thank him! . . ."*

There was a knock on the door.

"George? Can I come in?"

"Hey Hib, it's done! I'm just trying it out. You want to hear something beautiful?" Hibbie walked over to the cluttered table and examined the new contraption. He nodded and whistled and stood in admiration the way he always did with George's inventions.

"Here, clear the bed. I want you to listen to it." George had forgotten his hurt and his anger. Everything was out of his head except what was on the table before them.

"Can it wait? I want to hear, but I want to talk to you first."

Hibbie sat heavily on the bed, his brow wrinkled with effort, his eyes pleading.

"I want to explain something to you, George. About t-t-tonight. About me wanting to be the Bozo. I know you're mad at me, but you got to hear me out. It just came to me, see? With Wilson up there . . . p-p-pouring it out, something in me said yes."

George didn't want to hear this conversation. He had had enough. "Hey Hib. I'll play you "Yankee Doodle" on my car organ here. Forget it, will you? Wanna hear?"

"Wait a minute, George. No, listen. You're right about my father, what you said downstairs. But that's dead and buried, right? Now about this Bozo thing . . . We don't talk much, you and me, about my . . . you know, about my t-t-t-trouble. We don't have to, hey kid?" Hibbie smiled and punched at the shoulder nearby.

"Ummmmmph," said George to the storage battery.

"You see, I, just *me* by myself, I'm just this big lunk who can't talk right. So what's out there for me? Something to be avoided like an accident, that's what. Right? Hey, you know that. Haven't we always been a team, us against the world? Well, what comes along? This Bozo thing. I'm all painted up in the face so I'm not Hibbie the Stutterer. I put on a different voice so I'm not Hibbie the Stutterer. It's Hibbie who has the trouble, not the Bozo. See that, George?"

He heaved his big body from the bed and leaned his elbow on the table to be closer to the boy. In the cup of George's ear, he said, "Maybe I won't have my trouble then. Maybe I won't. I want to know what that feels like. What that's like, to be like everyone else, to open my mouth and out it comes. Like now. Only with other people, not just you and Joanie. What it's like to have it come out easy, instead of dreading opening my dumb mouth. For once, George. I don't care if it's insults I got to say. Hey, I got a lifetime of those stored up in me! For once, George. Understand?"

He stood straight. "So, whaddaya say, George? Don't be mad."

George had stopped tinkering and wondered at his own feelings. He didn't even know where the hurt was. Hibbie had the right to . . . Sure, but how about them together? The stuttering thing was never something between them, never bothered *them,* so how come Unc was sticking his neck out all of a sudden, leaving George to . . . ? Not that he needed Hibbie. Just the other way round. Just this morning, they were the two of them like always. Then Lolly comes along, and one, two, three, Hib is stepping out. Was that it? George couldn't get hold of what was happening, but something was. There was change in the air, a difference in Uncle Hib. Whatever it was, George wasn't ready for it, didn't want it.

"Aw, that's okay, Hib. Why should I be mad? Do what you want. I don't care." He picked up the pliers to start working again.

Hibbie pulled the tool out of his hand and banged it down on the table. George hadn't seen him so angry since that time in eighth grade when George was punched out at school for dreaming in the outfield.

"Don't give me that! I know you from way back, kid. I don't know what's eating you, but you've got something backwards here. I'm twenty-three years old, George! Almost ten years ahead of you. Twenty-three and never had a date two nights in a row. What are we going to be, tell me that? Two old men sitting in a room together? Remembering nothing? You like that idea? Something's gotta move, kid. You, too, I mean. Maybe you'll be a great musician someday, but you have to live in the world, too. You don't give, you don't get. Simple."

He broke off and paced restlessly about the room. "I'm scared—scared stiff. But I'm moving, and that's it. Fighting the chimp is nothing. I let you get away with that tonight. Fighting one of those animals is nothing. Being the Bozo is something."

He stopped pacing and picked up an old mike from the shelf and shook it without intention. He sighed heavily. "Yeah, the Bozo is something else. I d-d-d-don't know. . . . There's Lolly, too."

"Lolly?" George asked. "Lolly the Liar?"

Hibbie had drifted to the door. His hand was on the knob. "I'm beat, kid. Long day tomorrow. M-M-Mullin's Lake deliveries first thing and then back to the Carnival after. Lolly wants to come with us tomorrow, and I said okay. Sure she's a liar, and a lot more besides. But I'll tell you, you're missing out on a g-g-good thing there."

The door closed behind him. George picked up the pliers and stared straight ahead.

Chapter 11

Hibbie called up to him the next morning. "Telephone, George. Mr. Young from the Clubhouse."

George wasn't a morning bouncer. He always felt there were pieces of himself scattered to the four corners of the earth that he must gather in very, very slowly. He reached out a hand for his jeans on the floor next to him and pulled them on as if drugged.

He padded down to the telephone in the kitchen.

"Yeah?" he said in his sleep-hoarse voice.

"Mr. Young here, George. Sounds like I woke you up."

"Uhhh. That's okay, Mr. Young."

"Sorry about that. Indeed I am. Would you like me to

call you back? I wanted to make sure to find you home."

George could see the slight man behind the mild voice in his ear. A trim boyish-looking man until you looked close. A man who wore long Bermuda shorts and high socks and who always treated him courteously.

"No, no, that's okay."

"I just wanted to remind you and Hibbert once again that the Improvement Gala is next Saturday night. This year, we're shooting for some play equipment for the kids. We are depending on you and your uncle for the lights and sound equipment like last year, of course. Would you remind Hibbert for me, please?"

Mr. Young was being polite about Unc. He would prefer not to talk to him directly.

The light voice continued. "A twenties dance, George. Even a bit before your dear mother's time, I vow. We have a collection of the old 78's—the big bands, the sweet old tunes. Not like now with the . . ." He stopped and cleared his throat. "Instead of paying out good money for a band, how about you taking charge of the whole thing? I mean change our records, set up the amplification system, whatever there is to do. If you can stop in later, we can discuss the whole thing, price and so forth. Prom Night is the theme. A prom the way it used to be, lights strung around, big sound, gardenia corsages, the works. A *formal*, as we used to say. Maybe you can fit into one of my old tuxes, and we'll have to see what we can do about your big uncle. Big Hib, heh, heh. Is it a deal, George? You'll see me do my Charleston. That'll be a sight!"

Mr. Young laughed aloud. His voice had gained strength in the telling. George could see him hopping around like a cricket in those high socks and long shorts. He could test out those four amps he swapped for last Christmas. Set them up in the four corners of the big Clubhouse and wow! They'll Charleston right through the roof. He loved doing it, putting up the equipment, doing what he could do best.

"I told him yes," said George to Hibbie as they drove to the bakery in town to pick up the delivery van and start their rounds.

Hibbert became solid outrage. "For me? You said yes? Didn't you tell him I'd be busy? Next Saturday night, George. Don't you listen to a thing I say?"

The Bozo. Sure he had listened. "Yeah, but we promised! Ages ago. Didn't you yell at me last night, tell me I gotta get out more? Aw, come on, Hib, one night won't kill you. You can be the Bozo some other time." He didn't want his voice to shake like that, but he had to see who counted around here. He'd been thinking. It was pretty clear: Hib could be with him like he should be, like he always was, or he could choose that other thing. And what made him feel so rotten was that he saw what he was doing to his uncle, to Hibbie of all people. He just couldn't help himself.

Hibbie said firmly, "Next Saturday I'll be the new Bozo. Sorry, George. You can do that job by yourself, you don't need me."

Hibbert swung his old Chevy into the narrow alley between the bakery and the bank. George hung on to the rope that held the door on to the car. The delivery van was parked out back, waiting for them to fill the trays with baked goods.

Lolly was sitting on the hood of the truck. Her face was tilted to the sun, eyes closed. The heavy black hair was tied back in a ponytail, exposing the pale sad face. Instead of the cover-up dress of the day before, she was wearing white shorts and a red polka-dot halter. It made her body seem more slight and childish than ever. It was the bloom on her arm, the exotic hibiscus, the red matching the halter, the insistence of it, that drew eyes to her and gave her weight. George could suddenly see that. Something to make people think you're somebody. Something for nothing because you're empty inside.

But *he* wasn't. Without his music, would he be needing props too? No, there was a sense of something inside him, something solid like a fist. He knew he didn't need writing on the walls, graffiti on his body. Whatever it was, it made him catch his breath and chase away all the sour notes running around in his head. He put his hand on the wheel as Hibbie parked, and Hibbie covered it with his own.

Lolly opened her large dark eyes, and the life flooded back to her face. "Hey, here I am. I've been waiting for you guys!" She smiled. The voice, the smile . . . something opened in George like a door.

She jumped down and helped with the loading. Hibbie and George went back and forth from the bakery with full trays. Lolly crouched in the back, stacking the boxes and wrapped loaves.

They set off for the lake, Lolly between them as before. Hibbie sang his ratty old songs in full voice as if he were on the stage of the Met. He loved to sing, not because he had a good voice, but because he could forget about his stutter. He never stuttered while singing. And when he was feeling good, the truck rattled with it. George and Lolly were caught up with it and joined in when they knew the words or just lah-lahed the tunes at the top of their lungs.

They stopped at the Clubhouse.

"You going swimming?" George asked Lolly. She was

standing by the truck, her eyes on the lake searching the shoreline.

"I don't know. I think I'd like to explore today, walk around the lake or something if there's a path. Is there?"

"I don't know. You know, Hib?"

Hibbie didn't know about a path, but he was doubtful about her walk. "Lots of private homes around the llllake. They won't like anyone w-w-walking on their property."

"Well, pooh on that! You're going to tell me there's something else I can't do?" Hibbie took no notice of her show of temper.

"It's just a half day today. We'll be back here at noon, okay?"

They watched her to the water's edge, where she turned and soon disappeared in the thick brush that lined the lake.

"You want to stay here?" George asked Hibbie. "I'll see Mr. Young. I'll tell him."

"We'll go together," said Hib.

They found Mr. Young in the back bathroom with the lid off the toilet tank and a wrench in his hand. "Always something," he said when he looked up at George and Hibbie crowding the doorway. "Never-ending job of maintenance here. I dearly wish my people at the bank could see me as janitor now that I've retired. Heh, heh."

George told him Hibbie wasn't coming next Saturday, that he could do the job alone, don't worry. Nothing to it. There was a disagreeable moment while Mr. Young removed his pitcher's cap, smoothed the thin strands of hair across his scalp with a brown-spotted hand and stared at his wrench as if it had offended him.

"Ssssorry Mr. Young. I have sssome—"

Mr. Young cut him short. "Never mind, son; never mind

explanations. But it does leave me in a quandary. I doubt sincerely if you can handle this by yourself, George. Handy as you are for your age, I'll have to find someone else. But whom?" He closed his eyes as if the substitute were behind the lids.

George begged Hibbie with a glance.

"Jim Johnson is up Maine gone fishing, Mr. Young. I know that for a ffffact. And there's no one else around can handle lights but George here. He c-c-can do it absolutely. Right, George?"

George said, "Absolutely."

Mr. Young nodded a doubtful agreement and looked so put out that Hibbert was moved to make up for his defection.

"Anything I c-c-c-can do to help around here? I have the afternoon."

Mr. Young turned his pale eyes to Hibbie. "Tell you what. You get out in the boat this afternoon and cut back the weeds for me, and we'll call it square for Saturday night. The lake is beginning to choke, and I was about to seek help cutting back. What needs doing, needs doing now, I always say. If you say George here can handle the dance alone, and he gives me his solemn word, I'll have to go along with that." He pointed at Hibbie with the wrench. "I thought I had your word on that, my young friend. Never go back on your word, and you'll rise to the very top. Like the water in this bowl. Heh, heh. The weed cutter is in the shed."

As they made their rounds, the morning was still cool enough for a breeze to ripple the surface of the lake. A haze blurred the full sun, and occasionally a cloud would darken it. But by noon the sky was clear and the sun free to beat down on the roof of the van. Hibbie and George were relieved to return to the Clubhouse and park under the shade of the trees.

They searched the patch of sand for Lolly. They checked the heads in the water, even the Clubhouse itself. Nothing to do but wait. They sat on the wooden steps of the Clubhouse.

"Should we yell, do you think?" asked George. "Maybe she's still walking around the lake. She can't get lost, you know, not if she just walks around it. Shouldn't take more'n two hours, though. Think she'd hear us?"

"Too far to hear," said Hibbie.

They sprawled on the steps watching the action on the small beach, waiting for Lolly to show up. They got some sandwiches and a Coke from the machines inside and for a while sat with the food untouched, as if the notion of it would carry across the lake and bring Lolly back. Soon they ate, and when the paper was balled up and tossed in the trash, they went out back to the shed to get the weed cutter.

They wanted to get out on the lake. If she'd fallen asleep someplace, maybe she would hear them better out there.

The weed cutter was a long, awkward tool. It was like a broom handle that branched out at the end in a Y. A thin blade joined the arms of the Y forming the cutting edge. George tied two rowboats together and got into the lead boat while Hibbie stood at one end like a gondolier. As the rowboat moved along, Hibbie dragged the blade underneath the water, cutting the clumps of weeds that waved their soft tentacles just under the surface. Every once in a while, Hibbie, who had stripped to just his blue jeans, dove into the water and gathered them up, large armfuls of slimy weeds. He dumped them into the second boat like a harvest. George couldn't bear that part of the job. It gave him the creeps to swim through those green ribbons. They grazed his body like hungry living things nibbling his skin.

When they reached the middle of the lake, George shipped the oars, and they both cupped their palms like trumpets. "LOLLY," they called. Hibbie suggested they stick close to the shore, circle it in fact. They could then see into the bushes, see if she was there, maybe asleep, maybe hurt.

George realized he didn't know a thing about her, what she'd do. She could do anything at all, and he wouldn't know why.

"What do you think, Hibbie?" he almost whispered.

"About what?" Hibbie whispered back.

They had untied the weed boat and left it to drift in the middle of the lake while they explored the shore. George dipped his oars one at a time in the still water, pulling and then gliding. They floated without a sound in the shade of the elderberry bushes and willows overhanging the water's edge. The smell of wet bark, of the bank knotted with roots and rotted leaves, rose about them. They moved through a damp chill.

"Do you think something happened to her?"

Hibbie lifted both shoulders to his ears, his whole body saying, "Who knows?" "That Lolly!" said Hibbie, as if there were no words to describe her.

A thought grabbed George, wild, impossible. But how many times just yesterday did she talk about how she's going to kill herself over this or that?

"Hey Hib," he said. He looked across the water. All those choking, tangling weeds, ready to pull, to pull down.

"Hey Hib," he began again. "You don't think for one minute that she's, she's . . ." For the life of him, he couldn't say it. He waved a hand at the water as if to point out a culprit. No sooner had he said that than he thought, How silly, it's probably just another one of her tricks.

Hibbie didn't laugh at all, didn't think it was a silly question. He considered it, lips pursed, eyes sweeping the lake, his face gone blank. Then his whole expression changed as if swiped by a washcloth. "Aw, of course not. She's a swimmer! She said she's a good swimmer, remember?"

Just then, a stone fell into the boat, and George looked overhead. They were under a willow. Another stone bounced off the side. They were alongside a large spreading bush full of white flowers, and under the fountain of white spray, laughing, tossing stones, kneeled Lolly.

"That's what I call service. You sent the car," she said. When she saw their faces, she was immediately contrite. "Oh hey, I'm late I guess." She held up a wrist. "No watch." She scrambled to her feet. "I found a great secret place along the lake, and I spent most of the morning there. I was just walking back when I saw you looking and hid. I had a wonderful time! My place is my secret, and I'll never tell anyone where it is my whole life long." She laughed again. This was a new Lolly to them, relaxed and happy.

She had climbed in and they rowed out to the other boat to tie the two together once again. Hibbie dragged the weed cutter through the water. In the bright sunlight, with Lolly sitting there behind George, their earlier thoughts seemed absurd.

"Pa says you're invited for supper. Fanny's going to be there. Aunt Fanny, the Fat Lady. Pop says you're welcome.

You know he expects you to fight his chimps for him."

Hibbie said, "I'm not going to d-d-do that, Lolly. I'm going to watch Wilson, and then he's going to teach me the Bozo."

Lolly nodded. "Can I ask you something? Why do you want to? How come you want to put yourself up front?"

Hibbie stopped poling. Over George's head, he said to Lolly, "Ever want to break out? Know what I mean? Llleave yourself behind?"

George didn't have to turn his head. Lolly's breath, the "Yes!" that spurted from her, struck him like a stone. He felt invisible, as if those two were entirely alone with one another.

"Look at me," said Hibbie, low and urgently. "N-nothing in the world wrong with me. Got all the right equipment in the rrrright places. And yet—something gets done to me. Yes! Ssssomething gets done to me." He had turned from Lolly and was talking across the water as if to himself. "It's an it. *It* does it. Stuttering grabs me and I can't explain, I just know it's marked me, set me apart. Sometimes it leaves me alone, sometimes not. Persons . . . places . . . it doesn't matter. It waits—and pounces. It's like Mr. Ugly said. . . . I'm like an exile."

He seemed to shake himself awake, and to Lolly he said more directly, "It's a funny thing: Sometimes I can tell when there's trouble ahead, like seeing a roadblock or something. Well, I d-d-don't see trouble ahead being a Bozo. That's all I can tell you. M-m-m-maybe there'll be plenty of trouble when I get there, but it seems to me I got to try. I g-g-g-got to break out of what I am sometime soon. Or else I'll grow bad inside."

He gazed at the girl with simple wonder. "But you, Lolly. How w-w-would a pretty thing lllike you know about these things?"

"Pretty has nothing to do with it!" she burst out, as if the very idea made her angry. "Pretty doesn't stop you from having troubles!"

This was too much for George. The feeling of being an extra overtook him, as if he were watching something too intimate for words. He wanted out.

He grabbed either side of the boat and rocked it like a cradle. He meant to dump Hibbie and maybe all of them. Who cared? It would stop the talking.

Hibbie whooped and plunged off, coming to the surface with a mouthful of water to squirt at George. He grabbed the side of the boat to help tip it over, to get at George.

Lolly's shriek stopped them cold. "NONONONO!"

The scream shot across the lake like a volley. Mr. Young stood at the edge of lake with a megaphone. "What's the matter?" he shouted.

"Nothing. We're okay," George shouted back.

Lolly whimpered to them, "I can't swim. I don't know how to swim."

Chapter 12

Fat Fanny was delivered in the back of a battered pickup truck. She sat on the enormous pink chair facing the rear and never once turned her terrified eyes right or left until the truck came to a stop near the vans of Jeffers Jungle. The tailgate was lowered and the yellow forklift that trailed the truck across the field wheeled into position. The onlookers watched the proceedings with the same absorption they would give to steam shovels and building excavations.

The man inside the cab of the lift inserted the fingers of his machine under the specially constructed chair. His face was set, his mouth grim with the concentration needed for such delicate work. Fanny clutched the arms of her chair and closed her eyes. The onlookers held their breath as one person. No one said a word. Gently and slowly, the chair and its enormous passenger were lifted up and out of the truck and lowered to the ground.

George felt a cheer was in order as when once he saw a tug successfully nudge an ocean liner out of its berth on the Hudson River. But who knew what the rules were for having dinner with the fattest lady in the world? He glanced quickly around for Hibbie to see if he could catch his eye, but Hibbie was over next to Mr. Jeffers, standing there with his mouth open.

For a moment George and Hibbie gazed in wonder at the sight of one of nature's whims, like seeing the Grand Canyon or Niagara Falls for the first time. Then Lolly's mother stepped toward her and said, "Fanny?"

Fanny opened her eyes, and then her arms, and said, "Oy, what a trip!"

Under the folds of clothing, the soft boulders moved. George could swear he felt the shock waves pass right through his feet.

Mrs. Jeffers was a big woman. In her spiked heels and tight pedal pushers, she was almost as tall as Hibbie and about as broad. But next to Fat Fanny, she was a dainty stalk. She took one of Fanny's hands in hers and said, "Fanny honey, this is a real treat! I haven't seen you in a dog's age. How have you been keepin'?"

Fanny said, "I don't get out much anymore, Marge. Only for you and Ralph and your chicken would I do this. I stay in the show tent most of the time now. Whew, it's hot!"

Across her lap was a large pink bath towel. She mopped her streaming face with it and then swabbed her neck. Pink was everywhere, chair, towel, striped dress, and pink skin rolled and rounded and in constant movement. Like being in a room full of balloons, George thought. Only the small head sitting on top of all that didn't seem to belong, with its blonde baby-doll curls and dark piercing eyes fit for a shrewd pirate. The rest a rosy cloud.

"Where's my fan?" asked Fanny.

The driver of the truck handed her a large, round Japanese fan with a long bamboo handle. He said to her, "We'll be getting along now, Fanny, Johnny and me. Everything all right?" When Fanny nodded, he said, "Call us just as soon as you're ready, hear now?"

Marge Jeffers boomed, "Nosirree. You don't go anywhere. There's aplenty, so you just stay put." To Fanny, she said, "Sorry to hear Si ain't feelin' so hot. What's the matter with him?"

Fanny lifted her arms an inch and let them drop. "What can I tell you? Every so often my husband takes to his bed. He says nothing's the matter, just exhaustion."

I'll bet, thought George.

Marge said, "I said to Ralph here, 'Ralph,' I says, 'this tour we get Fanny and Si here for a chicken dinner or else. You know how Fanny loves your chicken,' I says. Joey, come back here!"

The chimp had leaped from her shoulder to Fanny's lap. Fanny shrieked, "Gevalt! Get him off!" Marge snatched the ball of fur away from the vast lap, where it clung like a hairy bread crumb. Again the towel did its mopping job.

Ralph Jeffers stepped up and told Fanny the table would be set up in a jiffy. They were just waiting to see where she was put. He introduced George and Hibbie. "I forgot your last name, Hib," he said, and they all waited for Hibbie to produce it. George's heart sank to his shoes. Always, always, saying his own name was the worst for his uncle. He felt his own face burn as, sure enough, Hib was stuck for good. Couldn't go forward, couldn't go back, like a car stuck in neutral. He got the Hibbert out, but the Whipple was going to stay his secret forever unless he could loosen the noose around his vocal cords. Poor Uncle Hib, his eyes bulged and his body shook like Jell-O, and all the while Fat Fanny regarded him with nothing more than curiosity, fanning herself and waiting.

Lolly broke it up. She went over and kissed the powdered pink cheek and did the introductions all over again. "Hi, Aunt Fanny. These are my friends, George Weiss and Hibbert Whipple. Boys, this is Aunt Fanny, the best and biggest Fat Lady in the whole world."

Fanny's sharp eyes were lost in the laugh. "Go on now, bubeleh. Bless your pretty little heart. You're an old flatterer." She tapped the young girl with her fan. "I'm only 564 pounds and I hear the Berek Cavalcade out west has Jenny Kopcho weighing in at 610. Well, what can you do?" she asked the universe. Then she told George and Hibbie she was pleased to meet them. "Shake," she said. The arm of softened overlapping balloons was held out for support. "Fanny Gulik. Fanny Gulik from Brooklyn, New York. Ever hear of it?"

Meanwhile, the table had been set up in front of her so she didn't have to move an inch. The white cloth was back on the table with the same chili stains of the night before, reminding George that anyone living in the shade of the chimp stink wouldn't be finicky about some food stains. Platters of fried chicken were carried from the kitchen van, forks sticking out of some of the pieces as if the murder weapons had been left in place. Bowls of string beans, corn on the cob and applesauce followed. A mound of mashed potatoes fit for a winter's skiing was set down along with a boat of pale gravy.

Fanny's chair was wider than the end of the table, more like a sofa at a banquet. Lolly and Mrs. Jeffers sat on either side of the guest of honor, and the others were urged to their places. George and Hibbie quickly grabbed the seats next to Lolly. Across from them sat Sam and Johnny, the two drivers. Mr. Jeffers, down at the foot of the table, said, "What'll you have to drink, Fanny? Got some of my iced tea ready, or will you have somethin' stronger? What about you, boys? Beer all around?"

Fanny watched Marge Jeffers heap her plate. "I'll have some of your iced tea, Ralph lovey. I could drink a pitcherful." The fan never stopped. George was stealing glances at her, trying not to stare, hoping not to get caught. She must have noticed, because she said to him, "The heat gets me. That's the worst," just as if he had asked. She turned her head of blonde curls to Lolly's mother to say, "Marge, it gets worse every year. Every year I suffer more. What's ahead for me, I ask you?" At the same time, she scratched behind her ear under the hairline with the handle of her fan. This dislodged what everyone could see was a wig. It tipped down her forehead at a jaunty angle.

"Does anyone mind if I take this thing off?" asked Fanny and removed it at once without waiting for permission. Exposed to the evening air was a damp mat of iron gray hair that made her look immediately older and more real. The face wasn't a bad one, just lost somewhere behind the billowing fat. Its finest and most singular feature was a patrician and commanding nose fit for a Roman senator. It sniffed the chicken on her plate. "Mmmmm. Smells good. Smells like heaven. You know, I was a woman grown and married before I learned fried chicken. My first husband, God rest him, showed me. My mama didn't know it came any other way but boiled. We'd have a houseful of relatives every Sunday, and my God, the food then. And the fuss over me? I'd be passed around like the bagels, my feet didn't touch the ground all afternoon. It's a wonder I ever learned to walk."

She picked up a piece of chicken from her plate and halfway to her mouth stopped, looked at it and said, "Ralphie, I always say you are good with chimps but better with chickens. You got golden hands as my papa used to say of my brother the violinist. And I hope to God you washed them before you tackled this."

Laughter erupted around the table, and Fanny winked mischievously at George. For a moment, he could see the cute little girl who was passed from relative to relative to love.

Fanny waved the chicken leg as a salute to the table and took a dainty bite. She returned to her subject. "It's true. I suffer," she told them all. "I can't hardly walk anymore, don't move from the show tent from one day to the next, sick of eyes, sick of faces, sick of knitting . . ." The list made her mouth turn down at the corners, and her eyes closed in woe. She reached out, groping the air for Lolly's sympathetic hand.

George glued his eyes to his plate, praying she wasn't about to cry. It looked dark and cool under the table. Why couldn't he take his plate and eat down there?

Ralph Jeffers' deep plain voice rumbled from the other

end of the table. "Come on now, Fan, cheer up. I know you gotta lot to complain of. Folks don't know and don't realize. But then too, you gotta remember you're the most popular attraction here at this carny or anywhere. No one can touch you for popular. Now do I speak the truth or don't I? And men? You have to beat them off, way I hear it. Tell these green boys about that!"

"True," said Fanny suddenly cheerful. Complacently she said, "I make everyone feel good, no doubt about it. The ladies love me 'cause they ain't me, no matter how much they need to diet. And the men?" The drumstick was pointed at Hibbie. "What are you? Twenty maybe? Twen-ty-four?"

"Yes, ma'am. Twenty-four n-n-next month."

"Just last week I had a proposal from a kid your age, be-lieve it or not, and let me tell you, I got a son that old. Imag-ine that?"

George couldn't imagine that in a million years. How did she ever have a baby? Talk about finding a needle in a hay-stack.

Fanny continued, "The stories I could tell! Yessirreeee, some like 'em big." She shifted in her chair and caught George goggling at her. She laughed aloud as if seeing clear into his thoughts. At that moment, he was thinking how he could reproduce the sounds she made when she changed her position. What instrument could sound wet and pink and fat at the same time?

"Hey, you there, sonny. Wake up!"

"Who me?"

"You're a funny one," she said. "Yeah, you. Are you with us or not?"

Marge broke in to urge her to eat. Others were already on their second helping, and she had yet to make a dent in the heap on her plate. This prompted Fanny to tell the whole table that her appetite wasn't what it used to be. "Si is worried sick. Guess what I ate already today. Go ahead, guess," she urged everyone.

George's devil woke up. "A buffalo," he said and nudged Lolly.

She couldn't help herself. "A whaleburger," she whispered.

"A flock of wild turkeys," said George straight at her.

"An elephant casserole," cried Lolly, carried away.

"That's enough!" stormed her mother, coming down hard. "Stop that! Lolly, shame on you. I apologize for her, Fanny."

The bath towel was in use again, mopping across the face and pushed under the neck folds until her hand disappeared. "No apologies, dear heart, none at all. Listen, they're smart kids, and in the early days, they wouldn't be far off. Today it was a tuna sandwich, but once upon a time, did I eat!"

Lolly stood up and pushed her chair away. As soon as Fanny stopped talking, she burst out at her mother, "Me! It's always me! My fault! I can't do anything right, can I? The lousy chimps can dump on your head, and it's all right. But I can't open my mouth without you jumping on me."

Mrs. Jeffers said nothing, but stared fixedly at her daughter as she deliberately pulled the little chimp from her shoulder to hug it to her. Her silence beat in George's ears.

Lolly picked up the nearest fork and held it towards her heart like a dagger.

"Is this what it takes?" she cried. "Is this what you're waiting for?"

She threw the fork down and dashed wildly across the field, going nowhere.

George was cemented to his chair watching her desperate run. For the life of him, he couldn't move, didn't know what to do.

It was Hibbie who went after her while the hubbub at the table continued. Mrs. Jeffers now allowed her temper to fall on her husband. "You hear that? You hear that language she used to me and you don't say a word, just sit there like always? She didn't learn that here, I can tell you. My animals don't talk fresh. She's out of hand, and you don't do a thing!"

"Oh hush up, Marge. The girl is just going through a stage." Mr. Jeffers reached calmly for another ear of corn.

"There, there, dear heart," murmured Fanny, patting Marge's arm. "Pay no attention. The girl didn't mean a thing by it, just having a little fun." She made a gesture with her head to George as if to say go after Lolly, go get her.

There wasn't any point. George could see Hibbie with her across the field, talking to the top of her head while Lolly looked down at the clumps of stubble at her feet. Then the two of them returned slowly to the table. Lolly slipped into her chair and picked up her fork without looking up. She seemed entirely calm once again. Hibbie swept an embarrassed smile around the table and also sat without a word.

Mr. Jeffers creased his weathered face. "You owe your mother an apology, girl. Let's hear it."

Lolly said "Sorry Ma" to some string beans.

"Sorry my foot," drawled Marge Jeffers. "You're about as sorry as Joey here. Moody is what you are. Up one day, down the next. Nothin' here suits you. Couldn't wait to get here, and now you don't want any part of us. I'm the one can't do anything to suit you, it seems. I can't keep up with you anymore, understand me? You better straighten out, young lady! That little show just now was sick!"

Fanny waved her fan vigorously. She said, "Now, now, dearest, give it a rest. The child is with us again, thanks to this handsome man here. What did you say your name was, dear?"

George couldn't believe his ears. She wanted Hibbie to go through that again? His uncle lifted stricken eyes to hers. There was a malicious gleam in those fat folds, and George realized he was looking at a woman who was enjoying herself.

This time it was Mr. Jeffers who came to the rescue. "Hibbert Whipple, are you or are you not going to fight my chimp tonight? I say to you *please,* and I don't say that to many. You can ask my wife. What do you say?"

Now what? Hibbie never could refuse anything to anybody. Quick, quick, think of something!

Lolly saved them both. "Say, Hibbie, don't you have a date right now with Wilson? I thought he was going to teach you the Bozo on his dinner break."

"What's this all about then?" asked Mr. Jeffers.

Lolly told him about Wilson leaving the Carnival.

"That so? And Hibbie here is the replacement? Does Wallen know about this?"

"Not yet. It's a real secret, Pa. Wilson's going to get Hibbie all set first. That's why we have to go now, remember, Hibbie? He's going to teach Hibbie, and then both of us, me and Hib are going to be the Bozo. Only Mr. Wallen doesn't know that yet, and don't you go tell him, Pa."

Her father pushed away his plate as if it offended him. He crossed his legs and looked across the field to the treetops beyond, sucking his teeth. He finally said, "I don't know about Hibbie here, can't answer for him. But I can tell you, missy, that you can get that idea out of your head. We'll go into this later, not with our guests here. Not with Miss Fanny at our table."

Hibbie stood up alongside George. "Sssorry about that, Mr. Jeffers. Some other night maybe. We have to go now. I'm going to be the new Bozo, so I'll b-b-b-be around." He went up to Fat Fanny just as if he didn't know or had forgotten that she was out to get him in some way just for entertainment.

"It was a p-p-p-pleasure meeting you. I hope the heat doesn't bother you too much."

"From your mouth to God's ear," said Fanny. She looked at him, suddenly genuine, no more games. "Good luck to you, honey," she said, and meant it.

Then she followed the three of them with her weightless and lonely eyes, as they leaped and ran across the field.

Chapter 13

The next day was a bright clear Sunday. The sun splashed across George's narrow bed and woke him. For the first few moments, he believed someone was chopping wood on his pillow until sense returned and he realized it was the banging of the screen door out back. There was a quiet in the house that told him he was alone, no one home.

He riffled through his head until he found some music he wanted to hear. Yes. Ellington. He put the music on a turntable in his mind and listened to it carefully at regular speed for a while. Wait. There was something in the clarinet solo that had something to say to him. He wanted to hear it again from the beginning, but only the intricate woodwind this time. He slowed down the record and blocked out the other instruments. Oh yes, now he could hear the building line, the slippy rhythm of it. His blood filled with the sound of it. At first he listened to what it said plain, but then, like a kaleidoscope, a little twist showed him other ways of saying the same thing. He left the line of known jazz and now followed a dance of sound no instrument could ever make. It was a dance of shining atoms, electricity made solid, swoops and hollows of purest noise, the color of white. He heard nothing else until the telephone downstairs cut through the music in his head.

He threw off the sheet to answer it, but then heard Hibbie's heavy tread through the kitchen.

"Who was that?" he yelled down.

"Lolly. She's coming over. Wants to practice with me. I told her we'd give her lunch."

George climbed back to bed and bent his arm across his eyes to block out the light. He wanted only to return to his music and to stop the swirl of pictures in his head. He saw Lolly and Hibbie practicing the Bozo act and himself trying to get Hibbie's attention only he couldn't. Hibbie spoke to Lolly over his head as if he weren't there, just like in the boat yesterday. At the same time, a tremor began to work its way up to his breathing. Lolly was going to come to the house, maybe see his room, his things. He must be going crazy. How could you want and not want at the same time?

He moaned and forced another record on his mind's turntable. He pulled the music over his head like a sheet.

"Hey kid! Want breakfast?" Hibbie stood in the doorway filling it up. The jumble George had been feeling suddenly welled up and settled someplace behind his eyes. They hurt. They felt swollen. Without taking his arm from his face, he said, "You're a cradle snatcher, you know that? You know how old she is? Fourteen. Robbing the cradle, you are!" He wanted shame to strike Hibbie to his knees.

Hibbie was aghast. "What are you talking about? I'm not after her! She's just a kid, I know that! What do you think I am? We're just getting together to help me out with this Bozo thing. I thought it was you two who were getting along. Besides, she wouldn't look at me. Not like that, she wouldn't. What would she want with an old man like me, a pretty thing like that?" He stopped and considered, frowned and shrugged and said, "Course not."

Over his shoulder, he said, "Get up and help me with the car, will you, George? I'm putting some hinges on the door, taking the rope off finally."

They spent the morning in the driveway working on the door like an old married couple, passing tools back and forth, holding and lifting and bending without the necessity of words.

It was almost noon when Lolly walked up the driveway.

Hibbie straightened and wiped his hands on a grease rag. His smile could have eaten up the world.

"You're all dressed up today," said George, sliding his hands down his cutoff shorts to mop up. Today she wasn't the little girl. She was different, taller, older. It was the shoes for one thing, wedgies, with her painted red toenails sticking out of them. She was wearing a flared blue skirt printed all over with red poppies. A white peasant blouse with a drawstring neck was held in tightly by a wide black patent leather belt that showed off her tiny waist.

"You look like Elizabeth Taylor," ventured Hibbie. Her mass of dark hair was loose around her face, framing it like a delicate shell.

"You really think so?" Lolly bent her knees to see her reflection in one of the car windows. She fluffed her hair and struck a pose. Then she dropped it quickly with a short and bitter laugh. "Ma said I look a sight. She's probably right."

She picked up the discarded rope that had once held the door together and wrapping the ends around her palms began to jump, chanting, "L, my name is Lolly and my brother's name is L'il Sis, we come from no place and we only eat . . ."

"Liverwurst," supplied George.

Hibbie beamed at them and said to George, "Why don't you show Lolly your room? Give her a concert while I get us some lunch?" He winked at George.

Lolly followed him upstairs. He opened the door with a casualness he was far from feeling. She stood in the doorway for a moment taking in the shelves of broken-down radios and motors, all the dragged-home paraphernalia of his passion.

"Wow!" she said softly. "What a place! The town dump without the smell."

"Exactly," he breathed. "Now just sit down for a minute. I want you to hear something."

She looked around helplessly.

"Well, just clear a space on the bed, dump that stuff on the floor. Okay, now listen."

She sat cross-legged on the bed, her face lifted to him, her dark eyes entirely his.

He knew a moment of purest joy. The last time he had a kid in his room, he was eleven, and Timothy what's-his-name broke his Garrard changer. This was different. Lolly would understand.

First he showed her his true treasure, the remarkable

car-horn organ. Then, without a pause, just as the last door-bell was pressed, he left the organ to go to his shelves.

He carried four battered old radios to each corner of the room. "You are about to hear a shortwave concert," he announced. He fiddled with each one until it seemed to make some noise that satisfied him. He motioned to her to stand with him in the center of the room.

"Now listen," he said, and she did. From one corner, she heard humming and clicking. From the other, she recognized the Morse code. The one nearest the window was speaking Russian, and the other just emitted squeals and crackles.

"This is a concert?" she asked, truly at sea. And then she seemed to realize by George's turn of head and rapt expression that she must be missing something. She, too, slowly turned in place. "What am I supposed to hear?"

"Just listen to the variety! Like a stew—a grab bag!" He wanted to open up her ears as if she were just handed them and had never heard anything before. He wanted her to hear that there were strange possibilities in sounds, just as eyes, newly opened, must sort out what colors mean.

She nodded at George. He took her hand and walked towards one radio and then the other, changing what she heard.

George whispered, "It's like a make-your-own sundae. An audio feast."

Lolly left him and went back to the bed. As she sat, she stared at him with such big sad eyes, he said, "What's the matter? Didn't you like . . . ?" He gestured around the room—his treasure, his life.

Vehemently, she shook her head. He mustn't believe that. "No, no, that's not it, George. No, no, it was wonderful.

I can't even say it. You have all this in you. . . . I didn't realize."

She drew her knees up, and she hunched over them to stare at her painted toenails. She rested her cheek on an upraised knee and said, as if talking to herself, "I don't know what's the matter with me these days, honest I don't. I keep thinking things will get better for me, and they don't. Look at you." She raised her face to George, still standing in the middle of the room. "You're younger than me, and look what you can do. Everywhere I look, people seem to know how to manage, know what it all means and what to do. Me? I'm just plain nothing. George, sometimes I get so . . ."

He squatted next to her, wishing he weren't hearing any of this. He never read anyplace that people die of embarrassment, but he felt it should be listed as a legitimate cause of death.

"Scared?" he tried. It was the best he could do.

It was enough. "Yeah, that's it, scared. Scared things are going to stay this way, that I'm going to be like this forever. Scared of what I'm thinking. Bad thoughts." She shook her head and closed her eyes. "You can't know," she murmured. "Nobody knows, and nobody cares."

George had a glimpse of the dark. A glimpse of something he couldn't understand or handle. One minute she's up, next minute she's down—what's the matter with her? She was wanting something from him, asking something from him. And all that made him want to do was run away. If that's what Hibbie meant by him joining the human race, then he didn't think he'd ever make it. Much better not to try.

Lolly looked at George squatting in front of her. She really took him in. She saw his uncertainty and fear. Immediately she jumped to her feet. She smoothed her skirt and changed her voice, her face, her everything. "Whew!" she said, feigning a bright smile. "Don't pay any attention to me! I'm just being silly. Just forget it will you? You're terrific, George. Really. Thanks for showing me. Let's go down. I always get hungry at concerts, and there doesn't seem to be anything up here to eat except junk." She was the laughing, sassy, teasing Lolly.

Hibbie had the table set and the tuna salad ready.

"I was about to call you. Whaddaya think? Ain't he something, my nephew?"

"Sure is."

George blinked at his big childish uncle who was so proud of him.

They sat at the old enamel table in the kitchen and passed the food around. Lolly looked around the kitchen, admiring everything, not seeing, or not caring about the old linoleum on the floor, chipped paint on the walls, the stained ceiling. Living in a traveling van gives you a different outlook, she claimed. You get to feel different about space.

She pretended she was a fine lady in a fancy restaurant. She curled her pinkie and said, "Pahss the bloody bread, eef you please!"

George jumped to his feet, ready to play. He whipped the paper napkin across his arm and with a flourish presented the plate of bread under her nose.

"For madahm," he said with a waiter's bow, and then laughed immoderately, relieved almost to hysteria by Lolly's return to the ordinary.

Lolly said to Hibbie, "How did it go last night? You know all about being a Bozo now? Wilson teach you like he said?"

Hibbie felt his chin as if testing whether it needed a shave. "Well, we w-w-worked on the plank some so it will hold my weight. And he showed me how to work the m-m-mike and all. I did my Bozo voice on it and it sounds good, real good. Wilson says I'm a n-n-natural. But boy, is Wilson good!" He shook his head in admiration and threw back his head to laugh.

"Remember the guy with the earring, George?" To Lolly he said, "There was this guy, big guy, wearing an earring. Wilson w-w-wants to know if it means he's engaged, and know what the guy sssays? He says no, it keeps his navel from dropping off."

"Very funny." Lolly wasn't about to change the subject. "But did Wilson teach you what to say and all? Listen, Hibbie, that's a tough crowd out there. You don't know what you're doing, they'll eat you up alive. You'll get beat up like the other Bozo, remember?" She pushed her plate away and held out her glass for more iced tea, frowning and thinking. She measured him with a look.

"You know, Hib, I just can't imagine you up there dishing it out. *I* could do it. Oh, how I could do it! You're too nice, too easy. You see, they're out to get you. And what it is, you get *them* instead. They're looking at you, wanting you *down*. And you just give it to them. Serves them right. Self-satisfied creeps."

She was intent and fierce.

Hibbie was pouring her tea during her tirade. He put the pitcher down and stroked her arm as if gentling a thoroughbred.

"Whoa there, easy now. That how you see it?" He was amused. "Well, that's n-n-not how I see it at all. I'm not out to get them, honey. Sure, I w-want to sting them a little, get them to want to drop me. Get them to part with their money, throw at me. That's the job. Size them up and poke some fun, sure. B-b-but the way I see it, this is not between me and them the way you have it. Nope, it's not."

His slow soft way drove her to cry, "Dammit, don't you ever get mad, Hibbert Whipple? Here they've been laughing at you all your life, and you're not mad? Not wild tearing mad? This is your chance, you big ox! Your chance to get even!"

George sat chewing, looking from one to the other as if watching a Ping-Pong match. She was like a gnat on a sheep dog. But she was right, he felt suddenly. He'd never thought of it that way, but sure enough, if he were Unc he'd be full of it, full of rage. He'd want to cry out and hit and get it out of his system. Where did it all go, he suddenly wondered? Never ever had he seen his uncle truly angry, so where did it all go?

Hibbie wrapped his big meaty hand around Lolly's forearm, enclosing it entirely.

"Mad? No, I'm not. I don't think so, 'cause I don't feel it. Never thought about it, I guess. It's not their fault, m-m-my trouble, is it? So who am I going to blame?"

Lolly said "Huh!" very sarcastically.

Hibbie nodded over to George. "Well George here knows what I mean. Whaddaya say, George?"

George continued chewing, feeling their eyes on him as if waiting for him to say something, waiting for his opinion. Well, he'd rather not say, didn't know, but was overcome at that moment by how different people could be. He never noticed before! There was one question, though, that was safe to ask.

"You think this is it, Hib? You think being the Bozo is going to cure you?"

Unc had tried everything under the sun and more, to get rid of what ailed him. Nothing worked for long.

Hibbie shrugged. "Could be, kid, why n-n-n-not?"

George gulped down his milk and stood up at the same time.

"See you later," he said to them both.

"You going over to the Carnival with me later?" Hibbie called after him.

"Nope. I'm going to the Clubhouse. I'll take the bus. Next Saturday's the Gala, remember? I gotta do some measuring."

The last thing he heard as he left the room was Lolly saying, "Okay now. Let's get it so you're not murdered. Time to practice. I'm a mark, see? I'm rough, rough and male, and you're the Bozo. Now what?"

For the first time in all his life, when George entered his room, it felt empty.

Chapter 14

In the days that followed, George and Hibbie were careful with one another. The lines were drawn even though it was only for a week. He and Hibbie were together most of the time, first at breakfast and then for deliveries. But George had never felt so separate from his uncle in his whole life. He and Hibbie were on different tracks, and if that's the way Hibbie wanted it, well okay.

The big man sat next to him in the van, tender in his talk and in his smile. Like always. Yet it wasn't the same; it didn't feel safe the way it used to. It was like missing some part of his body, a finger, an eyeball, some familiar part of himself he never gave a thought to but was now without. It felt scary, a little odd, as if he were fragile inside and had to be extra careful until something healed.

After deliveries, Hibbie patiently stopped at the dump so that George could seek the growing list of what he needed for the Gala. The work for the dance had grown important to George. He wrapped himself in it. When Hibbie asked, as he did each night, if George wanted to come with him to the Carnival after supper, George said no, he had too much to do at home.

He didn't see much of Lolly that week. She made the rounds with them twice more. Then on Wednesday, Dr. Pepper got sick, and Mrs. Jeffers gave herself over to his care completely. That meant Lolly had to set up, sell tickets for the show, and help feed and clean the cages. So she was busy too, though no doubt Uncle Hib got to see her every single night at the Carnival. George tried not to think of that or even of her. Nevertheless, often when he heard music in a plaintive minor key, Lolly came to mind.

What George was after those afternoons at the dump was mirrors. What he had in mind was a giant light ball. It wasn't that he turned down a juicy motor or vacuum tube lying around just begging for adoption. Sifting through the piles, he rescued perfectly good radios—except they didn't work. Or perfectly good electric clocks except they were broken. Or beautiful insulated copper wire attached to nothing at all. Ignorant uncaring people threw away those things just as if they were junk.

However, mirrors were on his mind. Sunday afternoon, after he had left Hibbie and Lolly, George had met Mr. Young at the Clubhouse. He was still wearing the baseball cap, though his knobby legs were now covered with tan baggy pants too big in the rear. He straddled a chair to watch George crawl around the floor tracing the lighting system. His pale eyes followed the boy's movements, and he spoke to him as if they were old friends.

"This prom, now. Well, well, the memories. I met the missus at our prom. Bet you didn't know that. Yes sir, I can see it plain as day. She was with somebody else that night. Let's see now . . ." His mild voice broke off as he searched upwards for a missing name that seemed to be lodged in the ceiling. Finally, with a slight cry, he said, "Teddy Goodman! That's who. Wonder what's become of him, had such a way with the ladies even then. Well now, Mimsy was with him, and on my arm that night was . . . uh! What's her name? It'll come to me in a minute. Well anyhow, there we were with two other dates, you see. Two other people altogether. I noticed her right away. She was gliding along the dance floor under the big colored light ball with Goodman's hand spread all across her back. I noticed he bent that patent leather head of his to breathe into her ear. Fancied himself a sheikh, I daresay. Well sir, I cut in. Bravest thing I did in my life. She just looked so pretty under the revolving ball of light. Like some kind of magnet, she was. I couldn't help myself. Know what I mean, son?"

He looked at George crawling on the bare wooden floor tracing the wiring, filthy, intent, a solitary and single-minded boy, not quite a figure who would know about the wild throes of abandoned love. He shook his head, "Perhaps not yet. But you will in the course of time, no doubt." He chuckled and shook his head at something he was seeing in his head. "I can still smell her gardenia corsage." More simply, he said, "We just stayed together, you see. Danced every dance."

George sat up, an arm bent across a raised knee, caught up in what Mr. Young was telling him. He had never before pictured him any different from what he was now, a fussy, pedantic, kindly man.

"I don't recall now what happened to my date for the evening, poor child. Left high and dry like that. Though I fancy I heard about it afterwards. No, I don't recall that. What I do remember plain as the nose on my face is dancing that night with my wife, Mimsy, for the first time under the big flashing magical ball up there on the ceiling."

Mr. Young swung his leg around and rose, slapping the back of the chair as if to leave the memories there.

"Mimsy's arthritis may keep us from dancing all night, but you can be sure as Satan she will be wearing a gardenia corsage."

"What were they playing?" asked George, seeing two twirling figures in his mind and needing the music. A tremendous notion was taking hold of him, as much a longing as an idea. No reason he couldn't make a mirror ball for the Gala Saturday night and surprise the old man. Please the old man. Such a funny way to be thinking. It was a cinch to do. He just had to glue pieces of mirror onto a big styrofoam ball, attach the ball to one of his little motors and hang the whole damn thing from the beams up there. He'd have to figure out a way to light it up, but that was no problem either. He knew he had everything he needed on his shelves or at the dump.

"What were they playing where?" asked Mr. Young, his eyes narrowing on a group of noisy kids at the far end of the spacious hall, crowded around the Ping-Pong table. He was once again the benign despot of the Clubhouse, checking on what was going on. "That night," persisted George. "What music were they playing for your first dance? Do you remember?"

This was a huge joke to Mr. Young. He threw back his head for a bitter laugh. He rubbed the day's growth of white hairs on his chin and said, "Why son, I can barely remember my own name these days. Pretty soon they are going to have to pin it on my lapel. And you are asking me to remember what they played back then? This was in the year 1922 if I'm not mistaken. Well now . . . hmmmmm . . . I'll tell you what we were singing way back then. 'Oogie Oogie Wa Wa' was a great song, not silly like those long-haired Beatles I've heard tell of these days."

"Yeah, sounds interesting, Mr. Young, but can you remember what song it was back at your prom? That first dance with your wife you just told me about?"

Mr. Young talked right through him. "Another song that set us tapping was . . . let's see now, how does it go?" Lowering his voice as far as it would go, obviously imitating someone he heard in his head, he sang, " 'Oh when my baby smiles at me,' bum de da bum . . ." He tipped an imaginary hat and kicked out a leg. Then he stopped short and looked amazed. "Why say! All this foolery makes it come back to me. Bless my soul, I do believe they were playing a waltz when I cut in on Teddy Goodman. Yes indeedy, oh, it was the biggest thing then, the most beautiful song. Wait. It goes like this. . . ." He sang a few bars in a shaky tenor. 'My wonderful one, I adore you,' da dee da, lah lah lah . . ." He broke off and impatiently said, "You can't get anything from my cat scraping. Come over here."

He led George over to the tinny old piano used for square dancing. It was on the other side of the room from the Ping-Pong players. Leaning over the keys, Mr. Young picked out the tune with an index finger, singing along with a word here and there. George heard enough to get it and then sat down before the keys. "Like this, you mean?"

From the single notes Mr. Young had picked out, he was able to play the entire song as if reading from the sheet music. It was just something he could do, like having perfect pitch. Somehow he was able to pick up what he heard and flesh it out, his fingers knowing the notes and chords as if rehearsed. He never thought much of it, just messed around on the piano at home, playing something he had heard or improvising music out of his head to work off steam. This kind of piano music was easy for him. He could play by ear as easily as other people could speak.

As he played, some of the group at the Ping-Pong table drifted over. Others stopped talking, their heads turned in surprise at what was going on at the piano. The players themselves stopped to listen, their paddles held in air.

George wasn't aware of the growing audience until he finished and a few of the kids began shoving requests at him.

"Do you know, 'I Want To Hold Your Hand'?"

"How about 'Hello, Dolly!'?"

His ears burning, George didn't turn around. He didn't know any of them. He stared at the peeling wood of the old upright in front of him and said aloud the words he was thinking. "Don't know any of them."

Mr. Young was gaping at him as if to say Well, well, will wonders never cease. What have we here? Then he took charge. By now the Ping-Pong table had been abandoned, and there was a group of teenagers around the piano, ready to hear more. Entertainment was scarce at the Clubhouse. "Hold on here. One at a time. This young man can play anything evidently. Just hum him a bit. You there, Helen." He pointed to a girl in braids, her smile glinting with braces. "How are you, honey? You have something you want him to play?"

" 'The Girl From Ipanema,' " she whispered.

"Yes, yes, child, but how does it go? Anybody know?"

The catchy song was begun by a few and taken up by several more, and before the line was done, George had slipped inside the tricky rhythm of it and was building. Ideas occurred to him as he went along, variations of the original line. So rocking was his playing that some of the young bodies behind him began to move and twist and turn in absolute and silent compact with one another and with the music.

George heard the bounding feet behind him and a feeling of power rose in him that caught at his breath and poured into his fingers. Hibbie and Mom never paid attention, they were so used to his noodling around, and wild horses couldn't get him to play for company. He wasn't prepared for this. Those feet behind him were moving because his fingers said so. He always thought his music separated him from others. Now he felt joined by it, the sense of connection so novel and delicious he felt he could play forever.

With this, a wave of self-consciousness washed over him, and he stopped. His blood beat in his ears, and he stood up and closed the piano lid. He mumbled to Mr. Young, who was standing next to the piano, "I gotta go now. Can I use your phone? Hibbie'll come get me if he's home."

"I won't hear of it, George. I'll drive you home myself. I want to talk to you, young man. I have a proposition to put to you. For now I'll just say a thank-you, for everyone I'm sure."

George walked through the space opened for him by the dancers, and heard what they said as he passed by. He couldn't help the bubble of pure pleasure that rose up and then escaped from him, lifting the corners of his mouth and spreading in waves of light to the four walls.

Chapter 15

All Saturday morning as they made their deliveries Hibbie fretted about the weather. It was a gray day, the sky overcast and gloomy, emptied of clouds or sun. It was the kind of day that meant to rain.

As they drove around the lake, Hibbie kept sticking his head out the window to check on the sky as if maybe the gray were only painted on the windshield. Occasionally there were spatterings of drops needing a few swipes of the wipers, but nothing heavy. When that happened, Hibbie groaned aloud. He also groaned when it stopped.

George tried to kid him out of it. "Make up your mind.

I don't know whether you want it to rain or not. What'll it be, so I can arrange it?"

"I don't know," moaned the big man. "I'm scared either way. If it rains, nobody will come. And if it doesn't, oh God! There I'll be! What did I let myself in for, George?"

George was so pulled he said something he was far from feeling. He said, "Don't worry, Unc, you'll be fine. You'll be okay, you'll see." Then, without thinking, he added, "And so what if you're not? We'll be back like before. Is that so bad?" He could have bitten off his tongue at the look his uncle gave him. He had just wanted to cheer Hibbie up, not make it such a big deal. Why did he have to look at him like he was stabbed?

Early that same morning, before they made their deliveries, everything George needed for the dance that night was brought to the Clubhouse and unloaded. Hibbie had used the van for this, packing in the radios, George's personal turntable, the stacks of records, the mirror ball, reflectors, cables, wire, everything. They shrouded the mirror ball with a draping cloth to keep it safe from prying eyes and then had to go all the way back to the bakery to load up.

At midday their rounds were finished, and by the time they returned to the Clubhouse, things were looking up. It was clearing, though they had heard on the radio that it might storm later that evening. The sun was hidden by heavy leaden gauze, but a rising brightness proved it was still up there and trying.

Mr. Young stepped down from the porch as they parked. "The key, George" was the first thing he said, holding out his hand for it. George had needed an extra so he could let himself in that morning, and Mr. Young had handed it over as if it opened Fort Knox. He took it back now and tucked it away carefully. He said, "The decorating committee plans to arrive here about six this evening to spruce things up. You'll have the whole place to yourself this afternoon. That do you, son? I'll see to it that no one bothers you. The Clubhouse is off limits the whole afternoon." He was gleeful and jumpy at the same time, the excitement raising a flush to his cheek.

"I'm nervous as a kid," he said with a deprecating laugh.

"Me too," said Hibbie.

"Me too," said George.

The three of them grinned at one another, and then Hibbie turned away to return to his van. He wanted to get right over to the Carnival.

"Wait, Hib!" cried George running after him. They stood for a moment facing one another. The lake gleamed beside them and sounded of deep-chested frogs, of the nearby rowboat groaning at the rope, of the plash of fish leaping and then slapping the water. The sun had finally emerged, weak and humid but definitely visible.

"I'll be there," said George. "I'll be there for the four o'clock show. I wouldn't miss it for anything."

Hibbie nodded, looked as if he wanted to say something and then didn't, couldn't.

"Do you know what you're going to do?" asked George. The idea of getting up in front of all those people and trying to be funny or insulting seemed so strange to him. And certainly strange for his big, goofy, sweet-natured uncle who was only good and wanted to be better. And now, because of that, because of something not his uncle's fault at all, he was about to do something that might be awful. The unfairness of it, the injustice, struck him and made the solid earth beneath him feel suddenly not so solid.

Hibbie lifted his shoulders in a shrug and then reached into a pocket to show George a piece of paper.

"I got it written out here." Hibbie was whispering as if telling a shameful secret. "Wilson wrote out some things for me to say in case I get stage fright. But I'm not worried," he said, worried.

"Oh, well, then," said George, "that's okay then. If you know what to say and all, it'll be fine." He tried on a confident and casual smile. "Well, see you there."

In the hours that followed, what George had to do was to place all twelve radios around the perimeter of the recreation room and wire them all up together. Then he connected them all to the record player he had set up in a corner. The records he played would then sound through all of the radios at once. They would act as speakers surrounding the dancers with music on all sides. He wanted them to feel they were in the very middle of a large dance band.

He went around and adjusted the volume and tone control of each one, covering one after the other with a cloth when he was done so that the decorating people would keep their hands off and feet away. He checked his watch and saw that he had time to mount his colored lights that would shine on his beautiful mirror ball. These were coffee cans that he had lined with aluminum foil and then wired up to hold a 100-watt bulb. He had covered one end with transparent plastic, red, green, blue and yellow. He found a ladder out in the shed and then nailed the cans to the ceiling. The mirror ball would be put up the last minute. He didn't want the surprise of it to leak out too soon.

127

Except for that and the last minute checking, he was set up for the night okay. It was time to catch the bus for the Carnival. His heart squeezed in his chest at the thought of his uncle sitting alone on a piece of board, a target for people's anger. What would he do if things got really tough for Hibbie?

On a now sunny Saturday afternoon, the Carnival was crowded. George pushed his way to the Bozo booth. Hibbie was already sitting on the plank, a fairly large crowd before him.

Despite his concern, George burst into an incredulous laugh at the sight of his uncle. He hadn't thought of how he would look. Why, it wasn't Hibbie at all! It was a stranger in a white clown's face and a ridiculous red nose. He had painted an enormous smile under black circles of big sad eyes. The effect was arresting, a mask of joy and sorrow at the same time. Hibbie was wearing his old work pants and a clean white T-shirt that had the word BARF printed on it. He was still dry. He hadn't been dumped yet.

There was a mark in front of him ready to throw. George recognized him as one of the checkers from the supermarket on Front Street, a big-eared guy who rang him up as if he weren't there. Big Ears must have said something to Hibbie.

Then Hibbie spoke and laughter left him. Coming out of the throat of his halting, sweet uncle was a voice he had never heard: grating and contemptuous, bitter and insolent. It was almost unendurable.

Hibbie, the Bozo, said, "Tell me. Tell me, tell me, tell me. Tell me all you know, mister. It won't take but a minute."

While the laughter of the crowd rose, the mark threw the

three balls rapidly one after another. All of them were wide of the target. He plunked down another quarter and bought three more. He was goaded.

While Hibbie's astonishing voice rose and fell in nasty cadence, squawking and hooting without sense, the supermarket man took more care. This time he hit the small circle at the end of the plank, and Hibbie went down into the bath. He shot up spurting the water from his mouth the way George had seen him do all the years of his life.

When Hibbie got back on the board, he laughed his own laugh with a contagion that swept the audience. And then as the Bozo, he jeered, "Oooh, the man's turned wicked. If I said anything to insult you, believe me, I've tried my best."

A man who looked familiar pushed in beside George. The jodhpurs reminded him. It was Mr. Wallen, the Carnival owner. The slick-haired, thin-faced man wasn't looking at Hibbie so much as studying the crowd, breathing in deeply through long nostrils as if scenting the mood of the audience.

Hibbie's voice didn't stop. It was as if he were testing a weapon, shooting it off in all directions, reveling in the power of it.

"Come on, come on, can't you smell it on me? Oooh mama, I need a bath! You there. You with the dog on a leash. Oh, is that your friend? Paaahdon me! Anyone here want to see how nice I swim? You mister. Yes, you. You look like you have an open mind."

The man he singled out smiled at his wife. Proud and pleased that everyone heard what that funny man up there said about him.

"You should close it for repairs," said the Bozo.

The man pushed his way to the front to buy some balls. Mr. Wallen nodded and then noticed George standing next to him.

"I met you last week, didn't I? I never forget a face. You're this man's kid brother, right?"

"Nephew. I'm his nephew," said George.

"Well, he's doing all right. So far so good. I was plenty mad, I can tell you, when I heard our Bozo was leaving us your uncle. If I could have gotten a last minute replacement, I would have. I remembered your uncle's uh . . . trouble. I'm still not taking any chances. We have to move on tomorrow night, so I've got someone lined up just in case. But I must say, he's doing okay."

Another giant laugh swept the audience.

"Better than okay. Tell him I said so. I'll tell him myself."

He noted the growing audience with expert eyes. "It's a funny thing," he said aloud, but not particularly to George. "I've been in this business a long time. Every once in a while a natural turns up with the taste for it. The taste and the anger. Where you least expect it. It happens. Takes me by surprise every time."

Hibbie had someone up front. From what George could see she looked ordinary enough, a regular person, a lady from town dressed as if for church, even wearing a hat. But when she threw, she had a mean right hook. It didn't hit the target right off, but it was close and very fast. What an arm she had!

She wasn't saying a word, and all the while Hibbie was doing his infuriating and unsettling yelping. What did it remind him of? George suddenly knew where Hibbie had gotten that sound: from the chimps, from the Jeffers Jungle animals. When the second ball whizzed by, Hibbie shut up and then in his normal voice said respectfully, "Whew! I want you on *my* team, ma'am." This drew a laugh but not half so much as when he added in the Bozo voice, "Is that perfume you're wearing or are you spoiled?"

Clang! The ball landed on target and down he went.

After an hour of this, he announced he was closing down for five minutes, and George ran around to embrace the soaking figure, choking with laughter and relief.

Lolly ran up at that moment, and when George was finished hugging his uncle, she also wrapped herself around the big wet body. They went behind the canvas partition where there was a cot and towels and a chamber pot. Privacy for the Bozo.

Lolly looked terrible. Paler than ever, she had dark circles under her eyes, her dress was stained, and her hair uncombed as if she didn't care.

"I was only able to get away the last fifteen minutes or so," she told them. "I could kill you, Hib. You didn't need any lessons from me! Why didn't you tell me?"

The wide mouth smiled by itself, the black circled eyes stayed sad. And Hibbie said, "I didn't know it myself. It just came out."

George said, "You knew it would! You said you'd be a different person, and you were. It worked!"

Hibbie turned his masked face to George and said in a wondering way, "A different person? I want to tell you something, tell you both something." He grabbed hold of a hand of each and pulled them closer. "I learned something today I didn't know before. I only *thought* I'd be a different person up there. But no, what was coming out of my mouth was all me. All those people out there? I could have eaten them up and spit them out. I just didn't know what was in me, what a bellyful I had to get out!" He reached for a towel to dry his hair. "Woweeee! What a feeling!" He was exhilarated and shaken by his experience on the plank.

George noticed he still hadn't stuttered once.

Hibbie swabbed his wet arms. "I got to get up there again. Stick around, George. We eat in an hour. Next free time I have is eight o'clock tonight."

"Eight o'clock," repeated Lolly like an automaton.

George told him that he had to leave soon. He had to be getting back. He told Hib to wait up for him or maybe come on over to the dance if he wasn't home yet.

"What dance?" asked Lolly.

When Hib reminded her about George taking over the Gala at the Clubhouse tonight, she said, "Oh. I forgot. I forget a lot of things these days." She tucked a lank strand of hair behind an ear. "I've been busy," she informed George. "My mother has a sick chimp, takes up her time. I'm taking her place."

She laughed at that in a way that made Hibbie say gently, "What's the matter, Lolly?"

The girl looked up at him and shook her head vigorously. "Nothing," she said. Then in a swift motion she was at the canvas partition. She lifted the flap and before disappearing said, "I don't know what's the matter. I just know I gotta bust out of here. Like you said once, leave myself behind. You know? Something's got to give."

She was gone.

Hibbie and George exchanged a concerned and bewildered look. And then Hibbie had to be the Bozo again.

In the middle of the next show, George left. It was almost six, and he still had work to do for the setting up.

As he pushed his way out of the crowd, the laughter followed him. But high above the throng the Bozo's voice rose, striding the air like a fury.

"Brains aren't everything," he told someone. "In fact in your case they're nothing."

Chapter 16

The old recreation hall was transformed. Full of flowers and streamers, it had been fussed over and spruced up like an old bridegroom. George waited in his corner behind the turntable.

Mr. Young and his wife were among the early arrivals. As soon as George spotted them, he sprang to the main lights, turned them off and started up the mirror ball.

It was entirely satisfactory. The Youngs and their friends stopped chattering and stood under the revolving multicolored light ball, looking up in delighted wonder. The men were mostly in white jackets over wide floppy pants, except for Mr. Young, who had unearthed an old and shiny tuxedo. The women dressed in colorful short skirts, long beads that hung almost to the hem and belts slung about some very broad beams. Hair was thinning or gray, stockings were full of old golf muscles, but there was an air of gaiety and expectation about the costumed guests as if indeed they had returned to their youth.

Mr. Young, his mouth still gaping, took a step towards George, who held up a hand as if to tell him to wait right there. He then went to the piano to play the same waltz Mr. Young had picked out with a shaky index finger the week before, the one he and his wife had danced to the night they met.

It was an easy thing to play, and as soon as he got the melody going, he was able to steal glances over his shoulder at what was doing out on the dance floor. Sure enough, Mr. Young and a small lady were clasped and moving. Others joined them, and one after another, as the guests arrived, they slipped right away into the old waltz, some of them with cries of recognition. After that, after the applause and his own awkward head-bobbing, George sighed with relief. The sticky part was over, and for the rest of the night, he could be invisible, able to concentrate on his records and electronics.

Mr. Young came over to his turntable, and while George put on a record, he introduced him to a homely and thick-bodied little woman wearing a long fringed dress and a circlet of pearls around tight blue curls. George thought she looked like a lampshade, but he noticed her husband handled her most tenderly.

"I'm sorry I missed you last year," said Mrs. Young in

a voice that dripped violin tones in George's ear. "My husband tells me you are a talented young man, and now I see you are clever as well. It was such a thrill for us to walk in and see that glamorous light ball, not to speak of that nostalgic waltz. What a kind boy you are to give us that."

George had never been called kind in his life, nor had he ever thought of himself that way. He had no idea of what to do with the compliment. Mr. Young saved him. One more second and he would have dropped to the floor, grunting and snorting, hiding his head under her dress.

Mr. Young said, "Look at that." He gestured to the mirror ball, gleaming as it rotated, raining large drops of swirling color on the dancers beneath. "It's a jim-dandy, George. Where did you lay hands on it?"

George was only too happy to explain, and after the clucks and chuckles of appreciation, Mr. Young held up an admonitory finger.

"All the more reason to pay attention to what I told you, hey George?"

"What was that, dear?"

The older man tapped the side of his nose and winked at George. "Oh, we have our little talks, don't we, young feller?"

"Sure thing, Mr. Young."

"Just you listen to my husband, George. There's many a young person owes him their schooling and lots more."

"Come along, Mimsy, and stop filling his ears about me. Do you have another waltz in that stack over there, George?"

George did. He watched the old couple back on the dance floor, and every time they smiled, he felt responsible. Now that he had included them in his work, he felt linked to them like the cable to his mike. He wondered what his mother would say if she knew that. He suddenly wished she could see this fancy dance floor, be here in a nice dress.

He watched the swirl of dancers. Every once in a while he circled the room, checking the volume and tone of his radios. He tapped the mike to see that it was on low level to avoid feedback. Soon Mr. Young was going to make a speech.

George looked about the transformed Clubhouse, at his mirror ball slowly revolving, winking its colored lights, holding the secrets of his music in its gleaming and constant movement. The music itself surrounded him like a cocoon, and he had a sudden and fierce wish that things could stay like this, that he would never have to leave this night, this place.

A cold hand touched his arm.

"Lolly!"

He couldn't believe his eyes. She was suddenly next to him, cold and shivery, in full Bozo makeup, red mouth, red nose, black eyes, T-shirt and pants. The Bozo.

"I'm so glad you're here! So glad, so glad I found you!" Her cold hand clutched tighter on his arm. The big black circled eyes looked about the warm, bright, festooned room, not noticing the few curious people who stopped to stare at the visitor before dancing away.

"What are you doing here like that?"

"We can't talk here!" she cried. "Please, George, I've got to talk to you! Let's get out of here quickly!"

"Out?" he repeated. "Leave here?" The words didn't make any sense. Everything in him drew back, repelled and frightened by her showing up that way, all edgy and out of control. He managed to say, "You playing some kind of joke?"

Under her mass of wild hair, she stared at him, eyes wide and desperate. "Joke? You think I would? . . . It was no joke out there on that plank! And when I . . . Oh, George, I couldn't open my mouth, couldn't say a thing! I thought I could, but I couldn't. Like a . . . Mama's chimps would have done better!" She broke off to laugh shortly and bitterly. "A joke? I'll tell you a good one. *I'm* the Bozo who was tongue-tied, not Hibbie. And all that laughing! It was horrible! So I ran home—to them, to my parents. And she. And she . . ." She trailed off and looked about her as if totally surprised at where she was. Seriously, almost confidingly, she said, "They're busy, you see. Too busy for me."

George's thoughts darted here and there like a rat in a maze trying to find a way out. Well, what was he supposed to do? Just up and leave everything?

"Tell you what," said George, trying to sound perfectly matter-of-fact, as if everything were normal. "I'll ask Mr. Young to open the office. There's a cot in there if you want. Okay? You wait there. Wait for me to finish. Calm down a little, okay?" He tried to laugh, hoping to lighten things up here, pull her out of it. Sure, maybe she'll sleep it off.

To his vast relief, she returned his laugh with a kind of smile. Something inside her had switched.

"Nah, never mind, Georgie-boy. I get it. You're too busy, just like everyone else, including the chimps. That's okay. That's allllright!"

She dropped her hand from George's arm. Then she rubbed her face as if washing it, smearing red paint, mixing it with the black so she no longer looked the Bozo but more like the mess at the end of a child's tantrum. "That look better?"

The record ended, and George jumped to put on another, nice and loud.

She had to shout over the music. "Never mind, George, don't be scared, little boy. I'll just wash this off outside. So long, my friend. See ya."

She was gone.

When she came back in, he'd give her the key to wait for him at his house. That was the thing to do! She'd be fine at home. Hibbie would come soon. No need to worry. When she came back in, he'd give her the key. She could catch the bus, and she'd be glad to go home and wait for them. Probably prefer it.

He kept his eye on the door, but she didn't come, she didn't come. The wind and the dark and Lolly were outside. The enfolding beat of the music, the light ball, were inside, where he belonged. His corner was besieged at the end of every dance by jostling, laughing people asking for one old record after another: a few that he knew, most he had never heard of.

" 'Toot, Toot, Tootsie!'? That's the name? You know what label? Just a minute, I'll check."

Was that a flash of red by the door? His breath caught in a flood of relief. Lolly was back. He had a hand up to wave and then saw it wasn't her at all.

Mr. Young stopped by to clap him on the shoulder. "Great dance, eh, George? The cat's meow, as we used to say." He stopped and examined George's face. "Anything the matter?"

"I'm okay," said George, and he smiled and nodded at the older man just as if an anxious fist hadn't formed in his belly.

He was bending over to check in his record stack for a request when he heard a commotion over by the door. He raised his head.

He was wet and blown and the Bozo. Like Lolly, Hibbie was in full mask, the white, red, and black churning in an eerie mixture as he passed under the colored lights of the mirror ball. He strode up to George, who was standing, staring at his uncle as if seeing a ghost.

"We've got to find her!" cried Hibbie.

George knew whom he meant. "She's here" was all he could manage. His lips felt suddenly numb.

Hibbie sat down heavily on the metal bridge chair. "Thank God!" he said fervently, and only then seemed to notice his wetness. He rubbed a hand down his bare arm, and the enormous red mouth creased upwards as he smiled at himself. "Where is she?" he asked. And then, as if relishing the breather from anxiety, he looked around him, for the first time noticing the attention he was drawing from the guests. "Guess I look a sight," he said. "Didn't even change. I was that worried." He nodded at the mirror ball. "Ball looks great up there. George, where is she?"

"What's going on, anyway? Lolly busts in here all crazy, dressed like the Bozo and says she *was* the Bozo and got stuck up there. Couldn't do it and got hooted off the board, way I understood it. Did that really happen, Hib?"

"Yes, yes, she took my place on my eight o'clock break all right. Didn't tell a soul. Poor thing froze and ran off to her folks, and that's when it happened."

"Come on, Hib, that's when what happened?"

"The Jeffers had the Jungle to do and the sick monkey on their hands and all. Guess they didn't pay much attention. Mrs. Jeffers said Lolly got into one of her snits and yelled at them. Said this time they would see the end of her. She'd show them! They'd never see her again!"

"Yeah, but so what? She said that before. *You* know."

Hibbie's big blackened eyes rested on George for a long moment. He shrugged his thick shoulders. "We were talking, see? Me and the Jeffers. I don't know how to explain, but right then, when they said about not seeing her again, it was like some devil from hell whispered the same thing to us at the same time."

George's eyes widened. "What did he whisper, Uncle Hib?" he whispered.

"That we should listen this time. We all felt it. So we searched and searched. And then someone told me they saw a Bozo getting into someone's car, getting a ride somewhere. So I came here to pick you up and go look. And now I don't have to." For the third time, he said, "Where is she?"

When he fully understood what George told him, when he finally realized that George, too, had turned her down, he turned an affrighted gaze at his nephew and ran out the door.

This time George followed the Bozo.

Chapter 17

The rain was slashing sideways, and the wind was up. George and Hibbie ran around the Clubhouse and then to the water's edge. Her name was torn from their mouths and lost in the tossed air.

It was George who noticed. "The boat is gone!" he cried. "She must be out there!"

They stood at the edge of the lake peering out, trying to see something other than blackness. Tiny lights circled the lake, random points of warmth and sociability from the scattered houses. There was nothing on the water to tell them whether Lolly was still there.

Again and again, they shouted her name.

"No use!" cried Hibbie in George's ear. "She can't hear us!"

He wrapped his arms around the boy, and George clung to him. For a moment they remained so, letting the rain pelt them.

George pulled away and at arm's length regarded his uncle but wasn't seeing him. Out of the panic, there welled up a way to reach her. There was a way . . . and he saw it and he knew it and he could do it.

He ran back to the Clubhouse, motioning Hibbie to follow. He pushed his way through the people gathered on the porch who tried to detain him with questions. "What's the matter?" "What's up?" "What's this all about?"

Mr. Young forcibly held him. "What's going on here?" he demanded.

"There's a girl out there. . . . She can't swim. . . . She took the boat. . . . She might, she said she might, she would . . ." George couldn't say the words.

Mr. Young leaped to them, aghast. "Might what? Do away with herself? Drown herself? In *my* lake? I'll call the police!"

When George reached his corner of the Clubhouse, he grabbed his microphone and indicated to Hibbie that he was to feed out to him the long cable that was attached to it. He turned the mike switch off and then turned the volume knob up as high as it would go.

"Everyone out of the room," he shouted. He wanted them all out on the porch, the further away the better. When he flipped the switch to *on,* he might have a dozen smoking radio chassis, not to speak of the many broken eardrums from the howl of feedback. It was a risk.

He ran back down to the water's edge with his mike. Hibbie was right behind him, feeding out the cable, completely mystified by what was happening but following orders.

When they were both at the water's edge once again, George turned the microphone switch on and held his breath. He might not be far enough away.

There was a grotesque *clunk* as the switch noise was enormously amplified, and a few shrieks from the porch at this. Then through the mike was heard the distinct sound of water lapping the edge of the shore. It was on and working.

Hibbie, realizing what George had done, grabbed the mike from his nephew. As he formed the word *Lolly*, anxiety for her rose up in him and choked him. It choked him where it always did, in his throat, in his starter, in his brain. It stopped him wherever the most precious secret of easy speech hid itself and stopped him cold.

"LAH-LAH-LAH-LAH-LAH-LAH!" he cried. The dancing refrain spread through the rainy night like a mockery of song, bouncing off the hills, beating its way back to him. Not *Lolly*, just *LAH-LAH*.

Behind him, the porch itself seemed to gasp, so precise was the audible dismay of the watchers.

Hibbie threw back his head and howled his frustration to the night sky. He thrust the microphone at George.

George looked as if he might drop it, as if it might be too hot to hold. He couldn't in front of all these people! He couldn't be so . . . so . . . What could he say that everyone could hear? No, no, he had already done what he could, it wasn't his business anymore, was it? He glanced around, but no one was near. Just the two of them at the water's edge. It was up to him. There was no choice, no ledge, no hole, no room to escape to. He was pushed out and off.

He said her name into the microphone as if she were sitting on the rim. Then he pictured her out there on the water, terrified of water but maybe more terrified of what was back here. For a single awful moment, he was able to put himself inside her skin, feel what she felt.

"Lolly!" he cried, his voice spreading out into the night, beating its way through the violent air. "Here we are. Me and Hib." Over the dark lake sped his voice, skimming the water, rising above the trees to the hills beyond. It was as if the thunderous voice of the storm were reaching out.

"Come back, Lolly," he cried out. "I'm catching cold out here!"

It might have been a sudden lull in the wind, or it might have been just the furious wish to hear. From somewhere out on the lake came a high thin scream.

Behind them, from the porch of the Clubhouse, the air was suddenly thick with cries of dismay. Above them rose the voice of Mr. Young, a frontier sheriff organizing his posse. "We need a boat! There's a girl out there! You there, Bob Roper. You live close by. Get your dinghy out there! Anyone else have a boat at the ready? Okay, Neddy, you be the backup. We'll be needing blankets. Get the cot ready in my office. You there and you there . . ."

The idea of rescue boats caught like a forest fire. While Mr. Young shouted his orders, the tumult on the porch thinned. Cars started up from the parking lot, and headlights fanned out along the lakefront. Soon crafts of all kinds set out on the lake, a fleet of bobbing lights from motor boats, skiffs, rowboats, dinghies, shells, even sailboats stripped of masts put-putted in the storm seeking the source of the scream.

"Yell, Lolly!" cried George into his mike. "Show us where you are!"

Dead silence.

Suddenly the night was rent by the spotlight from the police car. The pitiless beam swept the lake and picked out from the black water the empty rowboat, then the hand clinging to the side, then the drooping head.

Chapter 18

Inside the Clubhouse, the main lights were on, the Gala forgotten in the wake of real events. The mirror ball was still, the music stopped. The room was crowded with people all dressed up for a twenties prom, laughing, swapping stories, little groups forming and reforming to share with one another the experiences of the night. Some guests were still in the yellow slickers from their unexpected boat trips, rain clothes worn like badges of honor. A boisterous intimacy had spread about the old hall, born of weathering a crisis together, and of the giddy relief of averted tragedy.

At the rear of the Clubhouse near the piano was a door to the office. Lolly was in there.

Outside this room, Mr. Young was addressing the small group. They were waiting for the doctor to come out. The police had long since left.

"It was like Dunkirk all over again," said Mr. Young.

"It was like what?" asked George. He was leaning against Hibbie's arm, still shaky from the terror at the water's edge. He shivered and moved closer to his uncle, suddenly glad for the bright lights and the cheery noise of the party people. He wondered for a brief instant what had happened to his mike and cable and then put the thought away.

"How on earth would he know about Dunkirk?" said Mrs. Young. "That's ancient history to him, dear."

"Don't they teach anything in those schools anymore? There's a lesson here to be learned!" insisted her husband. There was a youthful eagerness about him, the events of the night had stirred his blood like a tonic.

"I was in that war," said Mr. Jeffers, taking the toothpick out of his mouth. He was leaning against the wall, his compact body looking odd and ill at ease away from his Jungle.

"Ah, then you know what I mean." said Mr. Young. He closed his eyes, an aging man in an ancient tux remembering an old war. "All those Allied soldiers, trapped by the Germans on the shores of France, ready to be slaughtered. All those young soldiers, boys really, doomed." His eyes opened to draw the small audience into his vision. His voice rang. "It was all those boats that saved them! It was the English who came to the rescue, comandeering any kind of craft they could, from tiny rowboats to giant yachts. Mr. Jeffers here will bear me out." He smiled triumphantly. "You see my meaning? Tonight, when the police held the spotlight on that poor child out there, hanging, just hanging on to the side of the rowboat, our club members were out there just like Dunkirk. I'd say there must have been more than a dozen craft on the water, all out to deliver that child, all those boats to the rescue. What a sight! Ah me."

"What's the lesson, Mr. Young?" asked George. "You said there was a lesson here. What is it?"

Mr. Young coughed and sent him a dry look under white bushy eyebrows. "Well, as to that, I'll think one up soon, and let you know."

The doctor came out of the room. He was one of the club members, his white jacket over his arm, his sleeves rolled up and his black bag in hand.

"What's the verdict, Walt?" asked Mr. Young.

"She's fine. Is the mother here?"

Mr. Jeffers pushed away from the wall and said, "No sir. Someone had to stay with the animals! Mrs. Jeffers is at home. I'm Lolly's father. I'm to know if we can take her with us tomorrow. We have another show to do upstate, and I'm wantin' to know if she's fit to take home with me now, fit to travel with us tomorrow."

"I don't see why not. I'd like to talk to you privately, Mr. Jeffers. For a moment, if you please."

"Sure. First, I want to see my girl."

"Certainly. I'll wait right here."

Hibbie said, "C-c-can we sssee her?"

"That will be all right. One at a time, please, and for just a few minutes. She's done in and needs rest."

Mr. Jeffers went into the office. As the door closed on him, Mr. Young said, "The child doesn't need another visitor, so I'll pay my respects through you, George. That was a double feat for you tonight, and don't think I'm not mindful of it. First the music and then your part in the rescue. All the more reason for you to take heed, take advantage of my proposal, do what I say." To his wife, he said, "I'm going to see to my guests for a while."

When he left them, Mrs. Young said to George, "Why the dear man intends to encourage your music in some way, no doubt. Am I right?" She beamed at him.

Hibbie was rapturous. "He wants to send you to music school! Lllike a dream come true! Wait till your mother hears this!" He lifted George off the floor. "What does he want you to do?"

"He wants me to practice more."

George was set on his feet with a thump.

"That's it? He wants you to practice? No music school?"

"What are you talking about, music school? You've been watching too much TV. He said I should definitely practice, and also he'll pay me to entertain at the Clubhouse, but I told him I already have a job with my Uncle Hib."

Mr. Jeffers came out of Lolly's room and looked around for the doctor, who was seated on a bench against the wall. He nodded at him and then went up to Hibbie. He stood in front of him and said, "I have a proposition for you, young fella, and I want you to listen. You see these?" He stroked his face and then his hairy arms. They were white-hatched with scars of old battles. "I'm not a man for words except when I'm talkin' to the marks. So I'll tell you once, and I'll tell you short. I need someone to take over Jeffers Jungle. Help me manage it."

He held up a hand as if forestalling a refusal. "I'll tell you my secret and hold you on your honor to keep it. Li'l Sis ain't but a tame one. He's as gentle and decent an animal as ever was. We got an act between us, so it ain't nothin' to work with him, to wrestle him. He won't hurt you. It's the chimps give me these, and I won't have you fightin' 'em.

150

Just Li'l Sis. Forget the Bozo, my boy. Wallen's got his replacement. So what do you say? There's a future in it, so think on it. We pull out tomorrow."

He nodded pleasantly to everyone. His last words were, "We got to be gettin' back. My missus is real anxious. So you talk it over with your folks, Hib, and let me know." He left the small knot of people to walk over to the waiting doctor.

George had listened to this with Hibbie, breathed with him, started with the same surprise at Mr. Jeffers' offer. He looked up at his uncle. "A future," Mr. Jeffers had said, and he saw that Hibbie wanted it.

Okay then, okay then. The sense of breaking loose from something still held. Father, brother, friend, so long. He said good-bye to Hibbie with his eyes. Hibbie squeezed his hand and nodded.

Then George went in to see Lolly.

She was on an iron cot. It usually had just the bare mattress, but now it was all made up like a regular bed. A white coverlet was drawn up to her throat, and her hair and wide eyes were the only dark against the pillow. Her lovely face was as pale as the pillow slip.

She lifted a hand and let it drop into George's.

"You look like Snow White," he said.

"And you're my dwarf Sneezy. It was that catching cold that got me, you idiot. Don't you know high drama when you're in it? Have you no respect?"

"Oh listen, Lolly, I'm sorry. Honest I am, to have shoved you away like that. I can't explain."

Lolly sighed deeply and studied the ceiling. "Ahhh, George. I've got so far to go." She lifted herself to an elbow and whispered to him passionately. "I couldn't do it! I tried

151

to, but I couldn't. I tried to push myself away from that boat, but I couldn't do it. I just hung there. I heard your voice. It pulled me back. I haven't told anybody. I told *them* it was an accident."

She lay back, suddenly tired out. In her normal voice, so thrilling to George, she said, "I don't think I fooled that doctor. He said he was going to talk to my father. I guess it's about what he told me. He said I need therapy."

"Oh yeah? What's that? Something fattening, I hope."

"Yeah. We'll serve it to Fat Fanny."

They smiled deeply at one another, and George stood up to go. He thought of the room outside, so full of life, so full of people. The mirror ball flashed by. He pictured it revolving about the entire room. I'll give it to her as a present, he decided.

When he reached the door, she said, "We come this way next summer, you know."

"Good. I'll teach you how to swim." What he thought was—Maybe then, maybe by then, I'll be ready.